Her heart did a front handspring...

...when she locked eyes with a familiar bronze gaze.

"Hey, I'm in a hurry, and need a cup of— Mac?" Rustic copper locks the same shade as the mums outside made McKenzie's usual greeting get lost in her brain. The blood drained from her cheeks as a man with an expensive watch stared at the old nickname printed on her well-worn name tag. If she imagined him thinner, added gold-rimmed glasses and a generous serving of freckles, she'd be seventeen again. And so would he.

"Ben Cooper." She found her words as she wrestled with a confused feeling of pleasant surprise. "I go by McKenzie instead of Mac these days."

"Well, other than that, you haven't changed." Ben smiled, and her breath got caught in her chest. She'd known they'd meet again. And with his father ill, she'd recently suspected it would be sooner rather than later. "You still wear your hair in a ponytail." Ben floundered, as if he didn't know what else to add.

It'd been twelve years, but McKenzie still knew what Ben was thinking despite the friendly charade.

Danielle Thorne is a Southern girl who treasures home and family. Besides books, she loves travel, history, cookies and naps. She's eternally thankful for the women she calls friends. Danielle is the author of over a dozen novels with elements of romance, adventure and faith. You'll often find her in the mountains or at the beach. She currently lives south of Atlanta with her sweetheart of thirty years and two cats.

Books by Danielle Thorne

Love Inspired

Visit the Author Profile page at LoveInspired.com.

The Doctor's Christmas Dilemma

Danielle Thorne

LOVE INSPIRED

INSPIRATIONAL ROMANCE

LOVE INSPIRED®
INSPIRATIONAL ROMANCE

ISBN-13: 978-1-335-59845-5

The Doctor's Christmas Dilemma

Copyright © 2023 by Danielle Thorne

Recycling programs
for this product may
not exist in your area.

For questions and comments about the quality of this book, please contact us at CustomerService@Harlequin.com.

Love Inspired
22 Adelaide St. West, 41st Floor
Toronto, Ontario M5H 4E3, Canada
www.LoveInspired.com

Printed in U.S.A.

For God so loved the world, that he gave his only begotten Son, that whosoever believeth in him should not perish, but have everlasting life.
—*John* 3:16

To Rob, Robert, Heather, Nicholas, Declan, Darren, Bradley, Crystal and Sam, for the love, patience and support. For happy Christmases you have given me, and the many more to come.

Chapter One

A crimson-red sports car zoomed into a parking spot in front of Southern Fried Kudzu, ruffling a few droopy mums slumped over a barrel on the sidewalk. McKenzie Price threw a glance over her shoulder at the noise, then turned back to watch Barney prep the day's beef patties through the pass-through window. "At least they were playing a good song," she teased.

"I'd rather hear 'Jingle Bells,'" the old cook grunted.

"When I buy this diner, we'll play 'Jingle Bells' year around," she promised. The bells on the front door jangled, and someone chatting on a cell phone dashed inside. McKenzie grinned at Barney as footsteps approached the register. The phone conversation stopped, and she turned with a bemused but polite welcome on her lips. Her heart did a back flip when she locked eyes with a familiar bronze gaze.

"Hey, I'm in a hurry and need a cup of— Mac?" Rustic copper locks the same shade as the mums outside the door stopped McKenzie's usual greeting from reaching her lips. The blood drained from her cheeks as a man with an expensive watch stared at on her name tag. If she imagined him thinner, added gold-rimmed glasses and a generous smattering of freckles, she'd be seventeen again. And so would he.

"Ben Cooper." She found her words as she wrestled with a confused feeling of pleasant surprise. "I go by McKenzie instead of Mac these days."

"Well, other than that, you haven't changed." Ben smiled, but Mckenzie's response caught in her chest. She knew they'd meet again one day. And with his father ill, she'd recently suspected it would probably be sooner rather than later. "You still wear your hair in a ponytail," Ben said, as if he didn't know what else to say.

It'd been twelve years, but McKenzie knew what he was thinking despite the friendly charade. This was the same place she'd worked at during high school, and the only thing new about her was she'd changed her nickname back to her full name to feel more adult. But the truth was, she was the same. No family. No career. Not even the little bookstore she'd always said she would own someday. And as Ben had just pointed out, she still wore her hair like she had all her life. Ben was a big successful doctor in Chicago now. Suddenly, McKenzie felt like someone had a heat lamp aimed at her head, and she was tempted to inform him she'd be buying the old diner soon.

"Yes," she said instead, "a ponytail works best for food service. How are you, Ben? Welcome home." His freckles had faded, his orange-red hair deepened to a gorgeous shade of auburn, and he was no longer skin and bones. It was a startling metamorphosis. "Is that your car?" She motioned toward the front window, trying not to show she approved of his new look despite the big-city inclinations .

"Why, yes, it is," he answered in a teasing tone. "The new Porsche. All electric. Would you like to go on a ride sometime?"

McKenzie gaped. Was he flirting? Ben Cooper didn't flirt. He studied. He worked. He avoided girls like the plague. At least, he had once upon a time. But he had a daughter now—sweet little Megan, who lived in Kudzu Creek with his parents. That meant he'd quit avoiding girls some time ago. "Um, no," McKenzie blurted out.

"Okay, but let me thank you for watching Megan while my dad was in the hospital." Ben's eyes looked darker than they used to be. Richer. "Mom told me you've picked her up from school a few times, too. Thank you."

"It wasn't a problem. She's friends with my niece." McKenzie suddenly needed to turn away to collect herself. The old diner that had been her rock for so long was now spinning.

"Are you sure you don't want to go for a drive?" Ben pressed. "It's been a while."

It'd been a long while because he'd left. Hurt strummed down McKenzie's spine. "It's not my idea of a relaxing ride through the countryside," she stammered with an echo of her old stubbornness. "Not in a car like that."

"I don't live in the country," Ben reminded her. The corners of his smile tightened. "Trauma centers don't grow like cabbages and cantaloupes do around here."

"Neither do race cars," McKenzie returned. They stared at one another, a thousand words swirling in a whirlpool of yesterdays and way-back-whens.

Ben cocked his head. "Do you still drive that old beat-up sedan?"

"My dad's car?" Snapped out of her memories, McKenzie countered, "No, I drive a *new* beat-up sedan. Compact, actually."

Ben's eyes flickered, and silence dropped between them like a piano from the sky. "So," said McKenzie, when it became apparent neither one of them was going to bring up the past, "did you want to order something?"

"Yes, a coffee," he answered in a tight voice. It sounded artificial. Not like her Ben.

McKenzie whirled around and bulged her eyes at the coffee machine. *Her Ben?* He'd been a dear friend, but he'd never been *hers*. His family was well-to-do, educated, and his parents had stayed together. Her family had been a train wreck. So they'd never been anything more than friends. Good friends. Until... A strange ripple of regret washed through McKenzie, uncovering small, sharp stones best left unturned. Ben broke the awkward silence by saying hello to someone on his cell phone. McKenzie exhaled. Surely doctors had voice mail.

When his coffee was topped off and sealed to prevent spills, she punched the order into the register as he waved a credit card in the air without breaking off his phone conversation. McKenzie ran the card, tore off the receipt and handed it to him with a stucco smile plastered on her face. He chuckled at something the caller said and gave her a quick wave goodbye with his pinky finger, like they saw each other all the time. "Bye," he mouthed. Seconds later, the flashy car outside growled to life and screeched away.

McKenzie's mind raced as she wiped off the counter in a robotic motion. Seeing her former best friend after all these years shouldn't have felt so uncomfortable, even if their last conversation had been tense and awkward. They'd spent almost every day of their childhood sharing their hopes, dreams and deepest secrets. They used to lean on each other through hard times. She shuddered, her nerves a tangled mix of interest and remorse. Ben had left for the city with big ambitions. She'd stayed in Kudzu Creek because leaving hadn't been worth the risk—not for a relationship. She hadn't been ready when he'd announced his feelings had blossomed into something beyond friendship.

The door jangled again, and McKenzie broke into a grin, anxieties forgotten. She waved at Ms. Olivia, her oldest and most faithful customer, who'd come for her sweet tea. Ms. Olivia always had a funny story, and McKenzie liked to make sure she was doing okay since she lived alone. She would have to worry about Ben later. Hopefully, Dr. Bentley Cooper of the big city of Chicago had forgotten and forgiven her for rejecting him all those years ago. He was just in town to visit his parents and little girl for the holidays and would be racing back to the fancy, prestigious life he'd left Kudzu Creek for in no time at all. She probably wouldn't even see him again.

If Ben Cooper was honest, there was a slight trembling in his arms and legs despite the outward show of calm. He caught himself putting too much pressure on the gas and slowed. It'd be awful to hurt someone on the road just because his adrenal glands were ricocheting between fight or flight. He stopped at a crosswalk for a dachshund, tugging its owner along, and inhaled a slow stream of oxygen to calm his nerves. Seeing McKenzie had startled him. That was all. He knew she still worked at the old diner and that they'd run into each other at some point. The country mouse who'd insisted she would never live in a big city had kept her word: she was still in Kudzu Creek. Still the same girl. Well, he corrected himself, she was actually prettier—in a mature, womanly way—and had retained her charming southern manners, except for the subtle dig at his new car. Ben scraped his lip with his teeth and frowned. Had nothing changed in her life since he'd left?

He circled the block of historic redbrick buildings in downtown Kudzu Creek and parked in the back alley of his father's medical clinic, still unable to pry McKenzie from the forefront of his mind. He'd assumed she would eventually settle down, just as he knew she was aware he'd had a wife for a brief time. Ben thanked God every day his parents had offered to take in Megan as a baby so he could finish his residency. But that was over now, and he was on his way up in his career. All he needed was a medical fellowship to become the renowned and respected surgeon he'd always dreamed of being. Coming home to help his father through Christmas was just a detour.

After shutting the car off, Ben grabbed his leather briefcase and headed for the back door. The cool morning air felt nice—nothing like the chill already in Chicago. He couldn't help but notice the clinic's brick was faded, the paint around the door's edges worn, and the knob tarnished from the humidity and rainstorms that had flooded over the gutters. Time had marched on in Kudzu Creek, even though he'd left as soon as he could.

He slipped inside. The clinic couldn't hold a candle to his hospital in Chicago: no clean, sleek lines; no glass or steel. *Let them laugh now,* he thought. Unpleasant memories of his childhood seeped in like an old wound whenever he dwelled on them. Would former classmates who'd jeered at his lack of interest in sports and clubs see his car around town and recognize the name on the vanity plate? Maybe one or two of them would visit the clinic and need his expertise. Ben wondered if that would impress McKenzie, then quickly shook the thought away. Their history was irrelevant now. He'd buried that disaster long ago—and besides, he only had to survive a couple of months back home in the town he'd tried to forget, and then he could be on his way.

"Ben!" Thin and pale, Kudzu Creek's senior Dr. Cooper padded down the hall and put an arm around his son. "I'm glad you made it in a little early."

"What are you doing here? You're supposed to be in bed," Ben chided him. "Three months off—that's what they ordered."

"Three is the minimum. Don't worry, your mother drove me over, so I wasn't behind the wheel. I remembered a few more things I wanted to go over with you a few minutes after you left."

"How's your blood pressure?" Ben pressed.

"It's fineDad grunted. "I checked it twice and took a legion of pills."

"Mm-hmm." Ben knew doctors made the worst patients.

"I have someone's file I need to show you." His father motioned toward his office, and Ben felt a rush of nostalgia when he realized the room he'd spent time with his dad in throughout the years would be his now. At least until Christmas. He shook his head in quiet disbelief. When he was young, he'd actually imagined working here someday, but that was before he learned of the limitless possibilities waiting for him outside the confines of their small town.

"Now, in case Ms. Olivia comes in unexpectedly—" Dad began, and a chuckle spurted out of Ben before he could stop it.

He put a hand over his mouth. "I'm sorry… She's still alive?"

"Yes, she's still alive! Her ticker's in better shape than mine." His father thumped his chest. "I gave her a machine to monitor her blood pressure, but she doesn't like it. You'll need to follow up, even though she promised she'd have her neighbor help out if she needed it."

Ben followed him into the cluttered office and sat in a vinyl chair on the opposite side of the desk. "That's important, Dad, but your quadruple bypass was no joke. All rest, no stress—remember? I only agreed to stay through Christmas so you can heal. You've got to rest *now.*"

Dr. Cooper lowered himself into his creaky swivel chair and reached for a pair of thick black-rimmed readers. "You're one to talk," he snorted. Thumbing through a file, he raised an accusing finger at Ben without looking up. "All those back-to-back shifts seven days a week. Traffic and crime and smog." He looked up pointedly. "You're already on antacids."

Ben shrugged. "Comes with the job."

"Not in Kudzu Creek, it doesn't. A year or two here would do you good."

"I like the fast pace of the city, and two months is the max. That's as far out as I'm subletting my apartment, and I should be hearing about a fellowship any day now."

His father glanced from beneath his thinning brows. "I know it's temporary, but are you sure? You always seem tired or worried about something."

Ben opened his mouth to disagree, but he knew his father was right. But that was life, wasn't it? No address guaranteed happiness. He certainly wouldn't find it playing the genteel country doctor in Kudzu Creek. That had been his father's achievement. The career, lifestyle and respect Ben needed could only be found in a big city like Chicago. "At least I'll get to spend some time with Megan during the holidays."

"Yes, she's happy you're here. We all are."

Ben's heart twinged, and he hoped it was true. His six-year-old daughter had behaved as if he were a complete stranger when he'd first walked into his parents' house, even though they FaceTimed once a week. She'd loved the doll he'd brought her...for about two days. Then her attention had returned to the menagerie behind the house that included several chickens, three dogs, two turtles and a fusty old donkey named Jiminy that brayed like the British were coming every time it wanted something to eat. "I miss Megan all the time. I appreciate everything you've done for her. For me."

"Maybe you'll remember what it's like to slow down and enjoy life while you spend time together. It might improve *your* health."

Ben leaned forward and took his father's hand—a hand he'd held on to for days in an Atlanta hospital just weeks ago. "I will, if you'll consider less gravy and a little more grapefruit during the holidays."

"You sound like my cardiologist." Dad squeezed back. "But I'll do it. They have a fruit bowl of something I can't pronounce at Southern Fried Kudzu."

Ben tensed. "Do you eat there often?"

"They cater lunch here every other week. Other days, I bring my lunch box."

Ben exhaled with relief. He'd rather pack a lunch than see McKenzie at the nearby diner so often. "Maybe I can have lunch with Megan at school one day when I have a break."

His dad nodded his approval. "Don't forget, we signed her up for dance lessons, too. I think it'd mean a lot to her if you were able to take her to her class."

Panic at another familial responsibility snatched at Ben's chest, but he remembered he was on a different schedule now—a tortoise's pace compared to what he'd been doing the past few years. "You're right," he agreed. "It will give me time to get to know her better." He stared at the calendar over his dad's head, wanting to bring up how much it hurt that Megan had acted like she hardly knew him. But maybe if he used his time wisely until the fellowship came through, he could return to Chicago relaxed, refreshed and reassured that his relationship with his daughter was back on track. She was his responsibility, and he loved her. He just needed more time before they could be a family. Well, half of a family, at least.

McKenzie crept back into Ben's thoughts, and the mortification he felt seeing her again colored his cheeks. He'd once been in love with his best friend, but she hadn't felt the same way. He rubbed his flustered face. He needed to keep those ancient feelings back in the farthest corner of his mind. He was just here to help out his father and connect with Megan while waiting for the next step in his life to come calling. Nothing else could get in the way.

McKenzie clocked out of Southern Fried Kudzu on Tuesday evening with aching feet. She'd worked at a frantic pace, as if expecting something to surprise her. Deep down, she suspected it was fear that Ben would walk into the diner again, but he hadn't shown up. She forced herself to relax as she drove home toward the sinking sun. Tree branches sagged alongside the highway. She kept the radio off, her mind in desperate need of peace to process her day. Last month, she'd asked the owner of Southern Fried Kudzu to hire an extra server, but nothing happened. She wondered if that was because of changes afoot. Mr. Hill had hinted he was ready to retire and sell the diner some-time in the near future, and McKenzie realized she had just enough money for a downpayment saved in her nest egg to buy it. She practically ran the place herself and could work any of the positions. Her two-year business degree from the local college in Albany, Georgia, had made understanding marketing, inventory and taxes a breeze. She was certain she was ready to be a business owner, but the recent growth in Kudzu Creek meant there were limited real estate op-tions on downtown's main stretch. She'd spent half her life at the diner on Creek Street, and it just made sense to take it over. She was glad Ben was around to see her get the business she'd always insisted she would have someday. He was just in time to see *her* dream come to fruition.

The dirt road to her family's overgrown property crept up, and she slowed to turn and bounce down the rutted lane until she reached her gravel driveway. The sparse lawn was bleached from last summer and spotted with riding toys, but the manufactured home was tidy.

Bailey, her six-year-old niece, smushed her face against a window screen to watch her climb out of the car. McKenzie snorted in laughter and heard a giggle in return when she hurried up the small porch steps. Bailey hightailed it for her bedroom as McKenzie rushed into the kitchen. "Don't lean out the window like that, Bailey," McKenzie called, dropping her things. She pulled open the fridge and reached in for a bottle of fruit-flavored water while her stomach rumbled at the smell of cumin and chilies simmering in the Crock-Pot.

"Okay, Aunt McKenzie. Do you want to see my new dance slippers?"

"Sure."

"What's she doing now?" came a hoarse whisper from the couch.

McKenzie stepped back from the fridge as she unscrewed the cap on her water bottle to greet her sister, Jill, who was lying on the couch. "Sorry, I didn't mean to wake you."

Jill sat up slowly. "Don't worry. You didn't."

"Bad day?"

"No, I'm just tired. Bailey had an asthma attack at school, and I had to go pick her up."

McKenzie sat down beside her. "Is she okay? Did you take her to the clinic?"

"No, she was fine when I got there. I gave the nurse some more medicine but checked Bailey out since I already had to leave work."

"Your supervisor didn't mind?" McKenzie tightened her jaw in concern.

"Oh, he minded and informed me my schedule is changing to include Friday nights." Jill groaned. "Factory jobs around here aren't hard to fill, so I can't take off in the middle of the day again—not with Christmas coming."

"You can call me. She seems fine now… And don't worry about Friday nights. I can take her to dance lessons when they change your shift."

"It's going to be right away." Jill sighed. "I knew she was trying on her new shoes, but I fell asleep waiting for her to show them off."

"It was nice of Tim's mother to send them." McKenzie leaned back beside her older sister and took a draw from her water, acknowledging the folded American flag and medals Tim Roberts had earned in Afghanistan. Her brother-in-law had passed away three years ago, leaving a stunned wife and baby daughter. Bailey was six now. McKenzie thought of Ben. His sweet little girl, Megan, and Bailey were in the same class at school and had become fast friends this year. When McKenzie had heard about Dr. Cooper's heart surgery, she'd called Mrs. Cooper and offered to babysit for a few hours when she was off work. She'd even picked up Megan from school a few times and let her play with Bailey in her room. Ben's parents had been very grateful for her help.

"Are you sure I shouldn't cancel her dance lessons?" probed Jill. "You seem distracted, too."

"I'm fine," McKenzie promised her. She didn't want Jill to worry. Her sister already felt bad for moving back into the family home McKenzie had taken over after their family had fallen apart.

"I can tell you're tired. Mr. Hill still hasn't hired anyone new, has he?" guessed Jill.

"He said he'll take care of it, but he hasn't. I don't know what he's waiting for." McKenzie bit the inside of her cheek, wondering if she should bring up Ben's return. "I didn't sleep well last night, either."

"Was Bailey up again?" Jill looked at her with remorse. "I'm sorry. Sometimes I sleep right through it."

"No, she was out like a light." McKenzie squished the thin plastic water bottle in her hands until it made a crackling sound. "It was just over a bunch of talk in town."

"I hope it's good news."

"Just interesting." McKenzie scrunched the bottle again. "Have you heard who's come home?"

Jill straightened with eager curiosity. "You

know you're my pipeline into Kudzu Creek. Who?"

McKenzie fought back a smile. "Ben."

Her sister was quiet for a second, then blurted out, "Ben *Cooper*?"

"The one and only. Except he's *Dr.* Cooper now."

"I'm glad to hear he's back, especially after his father's heart attack."

"I'm sure he's just visiting him," McKenzie said quickly, "and his daughter. In a fancy sports car and designer chinos. He's Megan's father, remember?"

"She's such a sweet little girl. I think it was nice of you to help babysit her while her grandpa had his surgery."

"We had fun teaching her how to dance and do cartwheels. No one's really shown her." McKenzie did not add that it should have been a parent or sibling if she'd had one around.

Jill pulled the knit blanket up to her chin and dropped back on the pillow behind her. "Dr. Cooper," she crooned, then gave McKenzie a mischievous grin. "Everyone said he'd never be a doctor like his daddy. Too quiet. Too shy. Always with tutors. And he drives a fancy car now?"

"That's him."

"It doesn't sound like the Ben Cooper I remember," said Jill. "Does he look different? Where'd you see him?"

"He walked into Southern Fried Kudzu like he owned the world," McKenzie drawled.

"Then he's come a long way. I thought he avoided town when he came to visit."

"I've never seen him in the past, but Barney told me he heard he's going to take over the clinic while his father recovers."

"And he came to see you? That was nice. Did he thank you for letting Megan come over?"

McKenzie nodded. "He mentioned it, but he seemed disappointed that I still work at the diner."

"You love Southern Fried Kudzu. There's nothing wrong with that. Besides, you've been there almost as long as the Hills have owned it. I don't know why he'd be surprised."

McKenzie whacked the empty bottle against her palm. "Maybe because I told him I didn't need to leave Kudzu Creek to get a fancy degree or a good job." She gave a soft laugh of derision. "I was going to start my own bookstore, remember?"

Jill nudged McKenzie's leg with her foot from under the blanket. "You do have a degree, and there's nothing wrong with staying in Kudzu Creek and buying the diner instead.

Who says we have to leave home to grow up?" She gave McKenzie a determined stare. "It worked out for me, didn't it? Even with Tim gone, I'm doing okay."

McKenzie gave her a sad smile. "Daddy always told us we wouldn't amount to anything if we didn't leave town after we turned eighteen, but I think he was wrong."

"At least he didn't sell the place when he went to Florida, so we still have a roof over our heads."

"You're right," McKenzie agreed. "Although it was Momma's to begin with, and it's still in her name. We have all the blackberries we want, there's catfish down at the creek, and a walnut tree in the backyard. Wherever she ended up, at least she left us this."

Jill sat back with a sigh. "And we have each other. Thanks for all you've done for me the past few years. I don't know what I'd do without you."

"I'm not going anywhere," McKenzie assured her. "Kudzu Creek has always been good to me, and it's home. Besides, Florida's too hot, and I'm too old to deal with another stepmother."

"And you don't mind having your sister and her little girl underfoot?"

"Of course I don't," McKenzie blustered. "I've saved a ton of money with you paying half the bills—and Mr. Hill is retiring soon, so I'll have the chance to buy the diner. Everything worked out the way it was supposed to, Jill. Soon I'll have my own shop, you won't have to work so much and we can stay together like a family. We're going to have a great Christmas. We *will* find joy."

"Doing what?" chimed a high-pitched cry. Bailey twirled into the living room in a leotard with matching pink satin slippers.

"Dancing," McKenzie replied. "With you."

"And my friends?"

"Sure," sputtered McKenzie in mild amusement. She couldn't help but think of quiet, serious Megan again. Ben's coming and going must have felt strange to the little girl. McKenzie knew what it was like to not have a bond with a father. And her mother had fled town and their family when McKenzie was just twelve, leaving her motherless. Her chest tightened. Ben Cooper needed to stay, she decided. He had a daughter here who needed him.

Her niece stepped forward and did a funny squat. "Is that supposed to be a plié?"

"It is one," Bailey insisted.

"It's lovely," said Jill.

"Yes, you're very talented." McKenzie winked at her sister.

Bailey tossed back her light bobbed hair. "I know. Are you going to take me to class next time, Aunt McKenzie? Momma has to work. Will you watch?"

"Yes. I'll pick you up after school on Friday."

Bailey clapped her hands with excitement. "You can braid my hair," she ordered. "And bring your camera."

"Yes, boss," sniped McKenzie with a grin. "We'll take lots of pictures and send them to Grandma Roberts."

"She'll love them," Bailey declared with the confidence of a boardroom president.

"That will be great." Jill smiled at McKenzie with gratitude. "I appreciate you doing so much for Bailey while I work this job until something better comes up. Tim would thank you, too, if he could."

"We'll be just fine," McKenzie assured her. "And Christmas will be wonderful. Now, feed me whatever you have cooking in that Crock-Pot because my mouth is watering!"

Chapter Two

Ben crawled out of bed at the sound of little feet scampering across the floor outside his room seconds before his alarm went off. He rubbed his eyes and checked his phone before remembering he was in Kudzu Creek; it wouldn't have blown up with messages overnight. Situated on the fringes of town, the restored farmhouse he'd grown up in received sufficient phone coverage, even surrounded by acres of pasture that backed up to a watermelon farm, so he knew he wasn't out of touch. He grabbed his clothes and headed to the family bathroom to get ready for the day that would be the first time he would drive his daughter to school. When he opened the door, she was brushing her tiny teeth over the bathroom sink. "Good morning, Meg." He searched her face for any interest.

She spit into the sink. "Hi, Ben." She squeezed past him and dried her hands.

He tried not to flinch as he dug through the linen closet for a towel. "You can call me *Dad*, you know." Megan stopped on her way out the door and tilted her chin up at him as if it hadn't occurred to her, then wandered out without a word. Ben readied himself, wondering if his mother's suggestion to take over driving her to school was a good idea.

Mom was at the breakfast table, urging Megan to eat a piece of toast slathered with muscadine jelly. She sighed but obediently picked it up and began chewing on it. "How do you like school this year?" Ben asked as he joined them. He was desperate to find an appropriate conversation for a first-grader.

"It's okay."

"It's more than 'okay,'" Mom chided her. "You love school. You're learning to read."

"Yes," acknowledged his daughter. She concentrated on her toast, lost in her own world.

"Do you have any friends?" Ben asked.

"Yes," she repeated, her mouth full.

"Don't talk with food in your mouth, honey," her grandmother admonished.

"Okay, Grandma. It's just messy." Megan wiped her mouth with an arm, and Ben chuckled, although he felt the sting of rejection once more. He gave his mom a sideways glance. Megan had plenty to say when she was talking to her grandparents, but for him, it was one-word answers in a bored tone. He searched for a question to interest her as he checked his watch. "Oh, we have to go."

"You have to work," observed Megan dully.

"Yes," he said in surprise. "We need to leave early so I can take you to school."

The little girl scooted back from the table. "I'm done, Grandma. Can you take me?"

His mother angled her head toward him. "Don't you want your father to take you?"

"No," Megan whispered. "I'll get my backpack." She fled from the room.

Ben studied his plate of toast and eggs and tried to act disinterested, but his cheeks stung like he'd been slapped. Megan was so much like her mother: Dark hair. Dark eyes. Cool. Distant. He exhaled, feeling his mom's attention, and tried to act like he didn't care. "S-she's used to you taking her," he stammered. "I don't want to upset the apple cart."

"I have errands to run anyway," Mom assured him. "I can have a talk with her, if you want. She's still feeling a little shy, so I'll drive her this one last day, and then McKenzie Price or I will pick her up later."

"Okay," agreed Ben nonchalantly, but hearing McKenzie's name on his mother's lips startled him. He wondered how often McKenzie filled in, he knew she'd helped out during Dad's surgery. "I should get going—but first, I'm going to wake the old man up and give him a hard time."

"Good luck. We appreciate you helping us out while you wait on your fellowship."

"It's fine," Ben fibbed. He wanted to say it was good to be home, but it wasn't. Kudzu Creek felt lonely and foreign. Everything had changed—except it was still a small hole-in-the-wall, without imported coffee, sushi, live bands or sports arenas. He couldn't even drive his car on a freeway. He scooted back. "See you tonight."

"Have a good day."

Megan walked back into the room, carrying a purple backpack with comets and stars on it. "Are you ready to go, little one?" asked her grandma.

"Yes, ma'am."

"Tell your father goodbye."

Megan continued through the back door,

only moving her chin slightly over her shoulder. "Bye, Ben."

Ben swallowed and decided not to correct her. "See you tonight, Meg." He watched her disappear out the door as if she hadn't heard him.

Later, after his first two patients at the clinic, Darlene peeked around the corner of the office and interrupted the nagging thoughts about his child. His father's faithful nurse of two decades waved a clipboard. "We have a little emergency we need you to fit in, young Cooper."

Ben looked up in surprise, ignoring the informal address that would have bothered him in Chicago. Darlene, out of habit, still treated him like a boy. "Is it my dad? He's supposed to call my cell phone." Ben's heart rate rocketed. He should have checked his father's blood pressure that morning and seen the numbers for himself.

"No, Dr. Cooper is okay," Darlene assured him. "It's our little patient Bailey Roberts. She had an asthma attack—second one in two days—and her mother wanted to bring her in." Darlene held out the clipboard. "Here you go."

Ben took the clipboard with a murmur of thanks. The nearest hospital was forty minutes away, and although his father's clinic was convenient for walk-ins, it was not an emergency room. He scanned the child's chart, then sat back and tried to remember if anything bloomed in Kudzu Creek during the early-winter season. Southern Georgia did not get cold like Chicago. The phone on the desk buzzed. "Yes?"

"Your next patient is here," announced Mindy, his father's secretary, from the front office.

"Roberts?"

"Yes, that's right."

He thanked Mindy and strode out the door. Filling in for his dad had not been as tedious as he'd expected; then again, that morning, his first patient who'd been seeing his father for twenty-five years had informed Ben he was too young to be a doctor. She'd promptly walked out, and Ben had given Darlene a small chuckle, biting his tongue to keep from saying anything. Not everyone in Kudzu Creek remembered him, and they weren't any more impressed with him than those who did.

He gave a sharp knock on the door to Room Two and let himself in. But before he could take note of his new patient, Ben found himself face-to-face with McKenzie, her sea blue eyes flickering like aquamarine gemstones.

"Y-you're Mrs. Roberts?" he stammered, ordering his heart to stop skipping at the surprise.

"That would be my sister. And you're Dr. Cooper's replacement, I hear."

"Temporarily." Ben pretended to be absorbed in the file he'd already read, embarrassed that he hadn't realized he would be dealing with the daughter of the late Tim Roberts and McKenzie's sister, Jill. "I'm filling in for him until he gets back on his feet—then I'm returning to Chicago."

"I know."

Ben looked up, but McKenzie avoided his gaze. She motioned toward a child about Megan's age with wheat-colored locks. She was pale, with her hand on her chest, wheezing quietly. "I'm Bailey's aunt," McKenzie explained. "My sister can't get away from work, so I took a couple hours off to bring her in."

"Let's have a look." Ben felt a wave of insecurity—as if his attending physician were evaluating him—and scanned Bailey's record again. "How are you feeling?" he asked the child in a gentle tone. The little girl looked scared, and he reached for her hand. She mumbled something, and he spent the next few minutes prodding her with a few questions that she was able to answer without becoming faint.

When he stepped back, he locked gazes with McKenzie, who'd been watching him the entire time. "She seems to be better now, but since this happened at recess twice this week, it may be time to talk about restricting some of her activity."

"Have you ever tried to hold down a cat?" McKenzie deadpanned.

Ben burst into laughter. "No, actually, I haven't—but I do recall you tried to put Peanut in a kitty costume when we were in eighth grade."

A small smile graced McKenzie's lips. "The scratches were worth it. He looked hysterical." She giggled suddenly.

"Who's Peanut?" rasped Bailey.

"A one-legged pirate cat," replied McKenzie dryly. She glanced at Ben, and he saw her fighting another grin.

He turned back to Bailey. "I think it's time you learn to use an inhaler that your mom or aunt can help you with. I'll be right back with your nurse, and we'll get things started." He faced McKenzie. "We need to come up with an action plan for the school. Does she get any exercise?"

"She dances."

Ben smiled at Bailey. "That sounds like fun."

"I'm really good," the little girl assured him.

"I bet you are," Ben replied. Behind him, McKenzie made a noise of amusement. He shuffled his feet, knowing it was time to go but wanting to talk more. Were McKenzie and her niece very close? Was she ever going to settle down? Did she think he still had a crush on her? His pulse skittered at the question, and he gave her a small wave as he bolted from the room. "I'll check on Bailey on her way out. It was nice seeing you again."

"You too," said McKenzie with a strange look.

Ben let himself out, releasing a breath he hadn't realized he'd been holding. The last thing he wanted to think about were the unrequited declarations of a silly young man. He'd been too serious, and somewhat delusional, to think the girl who'd been his best friend since third grade would follow him to college with his heart in her hands. At one time, he thought their relationship had meant as much to her as it had to him, but he'd been wrong. Some friends were never meant to be more; he knew that now. Ben's stomach rolled over, suggesting he skip lunch or perhaps warning him to flee from the clinic and keep going until he reached Chicago.

He shut the door to the office and leaned against it. Luckily, McKenzie hadn't mentioned what had driven them apart, and she hadn't made any references to the night he'd ruined their friendship. That was a relief. He closed his eyes and forced his shoulders to relax. Her niece needed attention, and she was lucky he was there to fill in for his dad. Ben suddenly needed McKenzie to know he wasn't bitter that she hadn't loved him back all those years ago and prove to her that leaving their small town to pursue a career in the big wide world had been worth it after all. Hadn't it?

Seeing Ben in the doctor's office had been an eye-opening experience. McKenzie tossed and turned all night, trying to merge the two Ben Coopers she knew in her mind, but by morning she was even more perplexed. Crossing her fingers that Bailey would make it through the school day, she arrived at the diner early and started a generous batch of biscuits. It'd been Mrs. Hill's job when the diner originally opened, and Barney had never developed the knack for it, so McKenzie had learned to make biscuits and tasty tarts. By noon, she was running around like a chicken, frustrated with Mr. Hill for not hiring the extra help she'd requested. The only other servers were Donny, who worked part-time after school, and Angela, a retiree herself, who came in at lunch; but it was not enough.

McKenzie rushed out a burger and sweet potato fries and returned to find Ben studying the menu board like it was a life-or-death situation. He didn't move an inch, only lowering his eyes when she rounded the counter. "Welcome!" She tried not to show her surprise. "Should I call you Dr. Cooper?" she teased.

He smiled. "Ben is fine. It seems my dad and his office aren't going to upgrade my title no matter how old I get, anyway."

"I hope he's doing better."

"He will be. He just needs rest."

"What can I get you?" McKenzie was relieved the tension of their first meeting had dissipated. Not that the second one had made her completely comfortable—just a bit more impressed…maybe.

Ben scraped his upper lip with his teeth, scowling at the menu like it was bad news. "There's a lot of grease in the food here, but there really aren't any other options close by."

"Try the fried kudzu," suggested McKenzie. "It has chickpeas."

"I remember when all this place had was coffee, tea and muffins."

"We still have those, but we added new items to the menu a few years back."

"Do the Hills still own it?"

"Yes." McKenzie wanted to tell Ben she planned to buy it someday soon, but she hesitated. It wouldn't impress him. "If you're worried about your waistline, we have the grilled-chicken wrap."

He sighed. "That'll do. There's no way I'm eating weeds."

McKenzie nodded, but inside something stung. Ben had never believed Kudzu Creek was good enough for him. She wondered why he allowed his daughter to live there. McKenzie bet Megan would give fried kudzu a try. She exhaled as she jotted down Ben's ticket and swung it over to Barney's side of the partition. The bald cook gave her a glance of acknowledgment. When she turned back, she remembered Ben's favorite drink. "Sweet iced tea with lemon?" Deep down, he had to be the same old Ben. She'd seen that Ben in the clinic with Bailey. He was probably a wonderful father, even though he lived out of state. She could see it in the depths of his golden brown eyes.

"No, *un*sweetened," he corrected her.

"Right." McKenzie went to work as if it didn't matter. After she handed him the drink, he headed over to a seat in the corner of the diner. She watched him go, wondering how to bring up the questions she had about Megan. Diane, the owner of Alabaster's Gift Shop next door, snapped McKenzie back to reality when she stepped up to the counter with her prim, arched brows. She pushed a little lock of silver-white hair behind her ear and gave McKenzie a sheepish grin.

"Good morning—and yes, I'm back for ginseng tea. I haven't replaced my teakettle, and you know I don't like to use that smelly microwave in the break room."

"We're happy to have you," McKenzie assured her.

Diane looked around. "I wanted to beat the lunch rush."

McKenzie checked the clock beside the menu board. "It's all uphill from now until school lets out. But that's a good thing."

"Yes, I know you're swamped these days, and it's good for me, too."

"Is business for the gift shop still booming?" McKenzie reached for the pastry tongs and headed for the glass display of goodies.

"Still climbing, after what I told you at book club last month," Diane informed her. She looked pleased. "Christmas should be an exciting time."

"That's amazing." McKenzie smiled, glad the holidays would bring someone she loved happiness. "I like to see small businesses succeed."

"So, what have you decided about yours?" Diane leaned over the counter on an elbow.

"About starting my own?" McKenzie picked up Diane's usual two strawberry-kiwi tarts to wrap and bag.

"You've talked about it for years."

McKenzie glanced furtively toward Ben before returning to the register and her friend's inquisitive stare. "Have you heard the Hills are thinking about selling the diner?"

"Yes, they're ready for total retirement. No more of this part-time business. She told me so at church."

"Mr. Hill said as much to me, too," McKenzie admitted. "I know I go on and on about opening a bookstore, which I'd love to do, but I decided Southern Fried Kudzu is too good an opportunity to pass up."

"You're going to buy it?" Diane asked in an excited whisper.

McKenzie nodded. "I've been here for years, and I know how things work. There wouldn't be any learning curve."

"But that means no bookstore in Kudzu Creek." Diane pursed her lips. "I'm a little disappointed."

McKenzie had to admit she felt a little sorry, too, but buying a bookstore was too risky. She'd have to invest her savings; the town might not support her; she could lose everything; and Jill and Bailey needed her. Without McKenzie's help, they might end up moving in with Tim's mother, who lived in Alabama. "The diner is a safe bet," she said.

Diane leaned farther over the counter. "I admit, I like having you next door so I can talk your ears off whenever I have a moment."

McKenzie chuckled, her mood buoyed. She looked across the room at Ben, and Diane followed her gaze. "Oh, the Cooper boy is back in town."

"He's filling in for Dr. Cooper while he recovers."

"Yes, I heard about that." Diane confided, "He wanted them to arrange other help, but they convinced him he needed to work on his relationship with his little girl. He can't just swoop in one day and take her back to Chicago when Kudzu Creek is all she knows."

McKenzie frowned. Why did Ben need to be convinced? Didn't he *want* to see his daughter?

"That *would* be traumatic—especially after her grandparents have raised her here."

"Well, a few months in town, and he'll be on his way." Diane gave her a wink. "Which is a shame since he's such a nice-looking man."

McKenzie chuckled. If Diane only knew how much Ben had been teased for his carrot-orange hair and freckles—not that he'd been any less nice looking back then, but now he was just… Her stomach gave a curious shimmy. He was mature. Confident. Successful. A temptation for any woman who was easily distracted— and without any roots.

"Did you know him growing up?" Diane asked.

"Um, yes," admitted McKenzie. Her cheeks warmed for no reason. "But this is the first time I've seen him in years." She glanced his way again as she took Diane's handful of cash.

"Keep the change," Diane murmured. She gave McKenzie a small wave. "See you tomorrow, if not before then."

Diane floated away, and McKenzie rang up two more customers while instructing herself not to sneak peeks at the corner of the room. She called an order back to Barney before she clipped it to the window. The line of customers began to build, and she sighed with relief when

Angela plodded in, grabbed an apron and wandered over to clear some tables. After noticing a few people in line checking their watches and phones, McKenzie decided she would call Mr. Hill again about the new hire.

A sudden commotion in the corner made her look up from the register with a start. Ben whooshed by, threw his half-eaten lunch in the trash and stomped out with his face as red as a radish. There might as well have been steam coming out of his ears, too. A crash of laughter swung her attention back in the other direction, and she saw Scotty Dougherty and Billy Johnston at a table adjacent to where Ben had been seated. They were laughing so hard their bellies and shoulders were shaking.

McKenzie's mind instantly rewound a decade. Dougherty had been one of the more exasperating boys at the county high school. He was in the crowd that liked to strut around campus, causing trouble, and he'd given McKenzie her fair share of teasing, too. She wiped her hands on her apron, called Angela over to handle the register, and grabbed a spray bottle and a towel. When she marched over to the snickering pair of overgrown men, she started to wipe down Ben's table, although she just wanted an excuse to listen.

"Hey, McKenzie," called Scotty before she could find out what had transpired. "Did you know Carrot Brains is back in town?"

She gave Scotty a side-eye. "Don't you think we're a little old to be calling each other names? And it's Dr. Cooper now."

Scotty took a clumsy bite out of his sub sandwich. With a mouth full of food, he said, "It's not like his daddy didn't have something to do with it. He couldn't have done it on his own, right?" He smirked at Billy. "Same old Carrot Brains with the same orange hair and freckles." Billy guffawed.

"What are you, blind?" McKenzie asked. "Ben's hair is a lot darker than carrots these days, and most women like freckles."

Scotty stopped chewing. "They do?"

"Of course they do. Who doesn't like a few adorable sunspots?"

Scotty stared as if he were processing her opinion like an old computer. "Well, he's still the same bookworm in the corner—only now he's a city slicker. No wonder he's single."

McKenzie gave Scotty a saucy look, wondering what his sweet little wife saw in him. "Girls like brains, too. It's the twenty-first century, Scotty. Catch up."

Billy snorted. "Just because he drives a sports

car and wears a stethoscope doesn't change anything."

She narrowed her gaze. "I assure you, it does, and for the better."

"His daddy paid for all that just like he always did," argued Scotty.

"No, he did not," retorted McKenzie, surprised at her tone. She realized she was holding the towel on one hip and the spray bottle on the other. "Ben Cooper worked hard to get into a medical school, and he paid his own way, too. That's why he always studied so hard. That's why he had tutors. He deserves everything he has, and it's not fair to resent him."

"Whatever," Scotty grunted and returned to his lunch. McKenzie stomped back to the register with an odd tickle in her chest. She tossed the towel and bottle on the counter and continued to the small restroom to take a five-minute break. She found herself trembling as she yanked the water faucet on. Her eyes glistened back from the mirror, and she splashed her cheeks and patted them dry. She wasn't just disgusted with Scotty and Billy; she was a little ashamed of herself. Yes, Ben had gone off to school and forgotten about her when she told him they could never be more than friends. Yes, he was now enormously successful, while she was still waiting on customers at the diner. McKenzie put a hand to her chest to calm her racing heart. They'd both made their choices long ago, so maybe she should take some of her own advice. Scotty and Billy weren't the only ones in Kudzu Creek harboring a little resentment toward Dr. Ben Cooper.

Chapter Three

Friday brought a stream of patients in who needed help before a weekend that promised to be cooler as low temperatures trudged in late to south Georgia. Deciding he did not miss the weather up north, Ben closed the clinic a few minutes early. He was surprised he was looking forward to taking Megan to her first dance class. The tiny leotard his mother had made her try on the night before made her look like an angel, and he was excited to see her in action.

He drove to the same elementary school he'd attended as a boy and waited in the car line until he spotted Megan. She seemed surprised to see him, even though her grandma had explained today would be different. She remained quiet, staring out the window after she was buckled in. After another soft, one-word reply to his question about her lunch period, Ben turned on the radio to play music he thought she'd find cool. They glided silently past the pharmacy and social services office until he spotted the one-story gray-brick building with the gravel parking lot his mother had described. A hand-painted sign on the front window announced they'd reached Miss Sherry's Dance Studio in glittery, gold letters. There was a hand-painted turkey with a red-and-green scarf, too. He pulled in and shut off the car. "I'm looking forward to seeing you dance today," he said with a bit too much forced cheerfulness.

"I don't know how to dance," murmured Megan. She pushed the door open and crawled out, lugging the duffel bag stuffed with supplies his parents had packed for the class. Ben followed her into the lobby of the studio. He pointed to the cubbies for personal belongings on one side, and Megan hurried over to store her shoes then skipped into the girls' changing room. There were a few plants up against the royal blue walls and a welcome desk in the center of the room. Beyond it, a large square dance floor with a mirror on the back wall and single rows of dark-stained bleachers on either side provided plenty of space to move around.

Ben joined the other parents on the bleachers

and plopped down to watch the class. A group of five and six-year-olds chattered like pigeons in the middle of the room, and he recognized Bailey Roberts, showing off her dance shoes. *So this is her class, too,* he thought, scanning the room for her mother. He hadn't seen McKenzie's sister, Jill, in years.

"All right, everyone. Gather around." Ben assumed the vibrant woman in the middle of the room calling everyone to order was Miss Sherry. She sported a few streaks of gray in her dark bun, and her pleasant face was accentuated by bright red lips. When she reached out a hand to Megan, his daughter stepped forward with rounded eyes. "Ladies and gentlemen, we have a new friend with us today," announced Miss Sherry. The flock turned as one and stared.

"I know Megan," Bailey announced. "She's my best friend at school."

Miss Sherry smiled. "That's wonderful, Bailey. Then you'll be her partner and help her get ready for the Christmas dance recital with us. Everyone, this is Megan Cooper, and she's starting class with us." She pointed at two small identical twins pushing each other for Megan's benefit. "This is Leo and Archer Ainsworth, and you may know their cousin, Emily, from school." Miss Sherry ran through the rest of the students' names, then said, "Class, let's show her how we warm up."

Bailey offered her hand to Megan, then searched the bleachers and grinned. Ben followed her gaze. McKenzie was standing in a corner as if she'd just walked in. This was a pleasant surprise. Apparently, McKenzie helped with her niece's dance lessons, too. She spotted Ben and broke into a smile. It made his heart bounce until he remembered the scene at Southern Fried Kudzu with Scotty and Billy. His old nemeses had acted like children, giggling and muttering insulting names to him under their breath. He'd made it worse by storming out—but later, after he'd reached the office, he decided to forget about it because there was nothing they could do to take his achievements away. Unfortunately, McKenzie hadn't seen that part. He squared his shoulders as she made a beeline for him. "Hi," she said after a few strained seconds.

"Hi." He pretended to watch his little girl, who seemed oblivious to his presence.

McKenzie slipped down beside him with a swing of her ponytail. It stirred the air with a tantalizing hint of pumpkin spice.

"Megan is a beautiful little girl."

"Thanks," Ben said quietly. He kept his eyes on the class. McKenzie turned to watch, and Ben realized as Miss Sherry began the first number that McKenzie could see him in the reflection of the mirrors.

"Have you been here before?" she prodded. "This is the first time I've driven Bailey over in a while."

He flitted his attention between her and Megan. "Um, no. Mom just signed her up. She thought it'd be good for me to bring her. While I'm here, I mean."

"That's good of you." McKenzie watched Megan eagerly perform a plié. "Will she stay in it after you leave?"

Ben shrugged. "Yes, if she wants to."

McKenzie looked at him curiously. "I would have loved it if my father came to some of my activities."

As if in agreement, Megan looked over her shoulder at Ben. He gave a quick wave, and something like appreciation brightened her eyes. McKenzie waved her hand wildly, and Megan grinned at her. "See," said McKenzie from beside him, "she wants to make you proud."

Ben almost choked on her assumption. "She doesn't even talk to me. She acts like she knows you better."

"Well, she's been to my house. I've heard all about her donkey, Jiminy."

"She said she liked playing at your place while Mom went to the hospital to sit with Dad. She hasn't done that before with anyone else."

McKenzie lifted a shoulder as if it was nothing. "We played games and made cookies. She and Bailey get along well. You will, too, eventually."

"I hope bringing her to dance classes will help," Ben admitted.

"Do you play together?"

"What?"

"You know, Ben. Play," teased McKenzie. "Like we used to do when we were kids. Play pretend. Make mud pies. Dress up cats."

Ben snorted. "We never made mud pies."

"We did," McKenzieclaimed . "You just didn't like to get dirty or wet."

"I don't think that was me." Ben swung his chin to study her and was alarmed at how close she was. He could follow the curve of her lashes around her jewel-toned eyes. He felt a tingle shoot down his arms. McKenzie stiffened as if she'd seen the jolt. He inched away and leaned forward to sever the connection.

"Well, *I* made mud pies," she mumbled.

"No," he disagreed, swiping away the electricity he felt, "you always wanted to climb into the tree house and read books sans shoes, in your mismatched socks. Remember?"

"I do remember reading together in your tree house and watching you do crazy-hard puzzles," McKenzie admitted. "I still don't match my socks."

"Sometimes we did homework."

"But it never lasted because we'd start talking."

Ben smiled at the memories. "And talking and talking. Until eventually, we'd sneak into the house and pillage the pantry for—"

"Cheese puffs," McKenzie finished.

"Cheese *balls*," corrected Ben.

She chuckled. "I haven't had cheese balls in years."

"Me, either." Ben's mouth watered.

McKenzie elbowed him. "Not good enough for you anymore, huh?"

"No." He grinned. She knew him too well, even though they'd parted ways long before he gave up cheeseballs.

"And you work out," she said, sounding matter-of-fact.

"Yes. I run, actually."

McKenzie laughed. "On purpose?"

Ben dropped his mouth open in mock offense. "What's so funny about that?"

"I just can't imagine you running. We avoided gym class like the plague."

"Band was a good substitute for gym class, and we worked just as hard—if not harder—during marching season."

"I suppose," relented McKenzie. "Do you still have the mellophone?"

Ben's mind raced back in time. They'd spent hours practicing together. He recalled their last band concert onstage, and then his mood soured. He'd been such a fool. "It's in the attic somewhere."

She didn't seem to remember—or maybe she was pretending—that the night he spilled his guts after the band concert had ever happened. Instead, McKenzie motioned toward Megan. "Maybe she'll take band someday. She can borrow my clarinet, if she ever wants to try it. Bailey's already decided on the flute."

"I wouldn't mind," Ben admitted. He could imagine Megan playing an instrument—maybe even a viola. They watched the class for a few minutes, and Ben wondered if he should bring up the scene at the diner with Scotty and Billy.

The music changed to country, and Miss Sherry ran the class through the same exercises with a different rhythm. Megan and Bailey joined hands and giggled as they tried to keep time. "I didn't know you had a daughter until she came to live with your parents when she was a year old," McKenzie began. "I mean, I'd see them at church…" She trailed off as if waiting for Ben to pick up his end of the conversation, but he tensed. His short-lived marriage was not something he wanted to talk about. After a moment, McKenzie cleared her throat. "So, how long are you going to live in Chicago?"

He sighed inwardly. She was trying. It wasn't her fault he'd embarrassed her in front of the whole school when they were younger. She couldn't help the fact that she hadn't shared the same feelings he'd had for her. A few parents around them clapped as the song petered out. If he wanted McKenzie to know he'd moved on, he needed to show it. Determined, Ben applauded and gave Megan a nod of approval. McKenzie whooped and called out, "Good job, girls! Way to go, Megan!" The child beamed back at her. "See?" McKenzie nudged Ben with her knee. "It's not that hard."

"What's not hard?"

"She's a little girl. She needs more than a nod."

Ben shuffled his feet. "I hardly know what to do."

"That's why you're here, isn't it?" McKenzie watched him chew his lip. "Besides helping your dad, I mean."

"Yes." Ben lifted a shoulder in a tight shrug. "But she's better off with my parents, as you can see. I'm never home."

"How come you don't visit more often?" asked McKenzie in a subdued voice.

Ben sat back, trying not to feel defensive. "I visit on holidays. They come up in the summer for a weekend."

"Wow." Clearly, McKenzie wasn't impressed.

He exhaled with frustration. "I'm done with my residency now, but I want to get a surgical fellowship to become specialized. Then I'll be able to get a job wherever I want, like in New York or Boston."

"That's wonderful, Ben," McKenzie said. "Those are big cities. I know it's what you always dreamed of."

He bristled at her praise, although he knew she meant it. "So you don't think it was a mistake, then? Giving up a life in Kudzu Creek to become a doctor?"

"If it's made you happy."

"I *am* happy." He saw a flicker in McKenzie's jaw. Now was not the time to rehash old arguments. He did not belong in Kudzu Creek.

"When are you going to start a business?" he asked, deciding to turn the tables. "That's what you'd always planned to do."

"I'm going to buy the diner," she replied. "It should go up for sale soon."

Ben thought of their long talks and childhood dreams. "I thought you wanted to open a bookstore."

"I changed my mind." McKenzie gave him a terse smile. "I already know how to run the diner."

"It is a rational choice," he said in a lone tone. And it was safe, he knew. McKenzie had clung to the side of the pool all her life. Especially after her mother had left her father when she was twelve. Then her father had remarried. Her sister had soon found someone, too. How McKenzie had handled her sister getting wed, he didn't know, but he bet she'd never leave town because that would mean surrendering all that she held sacred. She'd probably never quit the diner.

"It's what I want," she insisted.

Ben remained silent. He kept his focus on the dancing children. McKenzie could have wanted him back then, but she hadn't. She'd always gushed about her bookstore but had never done anything about it. He cleared his throat to dismiss his thoughts. They'd grown up, gone their separate ways. He was over it.

The air in the room felt heavy, until the speakers began blasting out a new song.—It was a melody he instantly recognized,. and it t filled his body with sickly heat as the singer crooned about coming home to the one you love. Ben stared straight ahead, trying not to show that memories from the past were flashing like strobe lights in his head. They'd played this song at their senior band concert weeks before graduation. After the final bows, he'd turned to face McKenzie, sitting in the second row with her clarinet. *Will you go to Athens with me?* It might as well have been a wedding proposal. He'd been talking up the University of Georgia all year, trying to convince her to leave Kudzu Creek and go with him. In his heart, he knew that going to college with your best friend would mean that they were more than friends—and it would signal the beginning of something new.

McKenzie had looked stricken that night. He'd watched her squeeze her hands, pretending not to notice everyone whispering around them. She'd smiled politely but later, in the parking lot, gave him a lecture for catching her unprepared, and she reminded him she did not want to go. And then Ben had done the unimaginable: he'd poured out his heart like a lovesick puppy until McKenzie jumped, red-faced, into her car and sped away. They did not speak to each other for the rest of the school year or throughout the summer. Their friendship since third grade had broken off abruptly, and neither one ever did anything to bridge the gap.

The ballad came to a wistful end, and Ben watched Megan and Bailey curtsy to each other and then laugh and embrace. He jumped up and walked over to the shoe cubbies, and he remained there until he could slip out the door with his daughter. The old ache he'd nursed for McKenzie had resurfaced against his will—and with it, a fresh, stabbing pain. He'd always suspected she would be the one who got away. But what did it matter? He may have come home for Christmas, but he would soon be back in Chicago, where he belonged.

Chapter Four

Having the weekend off did not lift the anxious cloud that followed McKenzie around wherever she went. In between chatting with Jill, playing with Bailey and catching up on laundry, she caught her thoughts drifting back to the years she'd spent with Ben. At the pivotal time in her life when her mother left, he'd been her go-to person. But after watching her parents' dysfunctional relationship, along with being surrounded by the drama of high school romances, she had decided that friendship was the way to go. Ben had enjoyed dissecting the guys who'd shown an interest in her to the point where it seemed the only men worth anything were between the covers of a book. But through it all, he'd always been there. Likewise, she had listened to his frustrations when he vented about his grades and choked up over the constant bullying over the fact that he was smart and a doctor's son. And of course, there were those tangerine locks that had plagued him until he reached high school, when they darkened somewhat—although not to the interesting rustic shade of bronze they were now.

A quiver ran down her spine, and McKenzie glanced at her reflection in the car's rearview mirror as she pulled into a small, narrow parking spot behind the diner. She'd worn her hair up to church the day before and put on a nice fitted skirt—something she hadn't done in a long time. She admitted it wasn't just because she'd wanted Ben to think she had done something with herself—it was because she wondered if he thought she'd aged well, too.

She pursed her lips and exhaled, climbing out of the car with an eye roll. What did it matter in the long run? She said no a long time ago because she'd been bound and determined not to run off from Kudzu Creek like her mother, and she would never leave her sister behind. Or her friends. Her little home. Everything she'd ever known.

McKenzie bit her lip as she hurried inside, asking herself for the millionth time if she'd made the right decision. It was silly to even wonder about it, because in a few weeks, Ben would be on his way to Chicago and the hospital he'd made his number one priority since he left. She blinked as more memories flooded her mind. Growing up, a few kids had made fun of his father for being a country doctor, saying he wouldn't make it in a real hospital. It had lit a fire in Ben, and he decided to become a surgeon—the best in the country, so they'd hear about it one day.

She allowed a faint smile at the tenderrecollection . He'd certainly done it. The only mountain left for him to conquer was…well, his little girl. He'd seemed enamored with her at dance class, and yet he lived so far away. McKenzie didn't understand it.

She stopped in surprise when she spotted Barney standing at attention at the break room door with his apron in his hands. He sent her a look that made her slow to a stop. A low, droning voice came from inside the room, and to her shock, Barney grunted, "Yes, sir," and then turned on his heel. He curled one side of his nose in an expression that put McKenzie on high alert as she eased into the room, confused and expecting to see Mr. Hill.

She hoped he was there with good news. Instead, a diminutive man with a receding hairline, dressed in an unappetizing shade of brown, stood behind the break room table with hands on his hips as if he'd just finished a lecture. He looked like an overripe peach. McKenzie caught herself gawking, her mind trying to sort out the situation.

"Ah," he said, as if continuing a conversation they'd never begun, "you must be Miss Price."

"Yes, I'm McKenzie."

The man looked down at an expensive-looking tablet in his hands. "Mmm," he murmured as if what she'd said needed consideration.

She slanted her head. "I'm sorry. Mr. Hill didn't mention anyone coming in."

"Didn't he?" The new arrival didn't look up from the screen he was perusing.

"No." McKenzie felt her blood pressure rise but realized there was no reason to feel intimidated. She'd been running Southern Fried Kudzu for years. "And you are?"

He looked up as if she'd asked to see some identification, and the tablet dropped to his side. He dipped his chin and gave a slight bow. "Maurice Mayer."

"I see," said McKenzie, when his dull brown stare seemed to expect her to recognize his name. Finally, he appeared to comprehend her confusion.

"I'm the new manager." He exhaled noisily, as if he'd just finished a workout. "Mr. Hill hired me to run things so that he doesn't have to worry about it anymore."

After thawing from the shock, McKenzie sputtered, "Barney and I have managed the business pretty much on our own for years, and I'm lead supervisor…"

Mayer scrolled through something on the tablet's screen, and McKenzie narrowed her eyes, wondering what on earth he could be looking for. She tried to remain calm, although a vortex was forming in the pit of her stomach. "Mr. Hill comes in a couple of times a month to pick up paperwork and see the books, she added.

"It says here you put in more than forty hours a week." Mayer was not using the team clipboard or accounting books stacked in the corner; he was glued to the mysterious information on his electronic device.

McKenzie bristled. "About fifty, give or take."

"And get paid overtime?" Mayer made it sound like a crime.

McKenzie sucked in a shaky breath. "I'm sorry, Mr. Mayer, but I was under the impression Mr. Hill was going to hire another full-time server."

The man chortled as if she'd told a bad joke.

"With you and the cook working so many hours, there was no real need—or extra budget—for it."

"But we're swamped," replied McKenzie in surprise. "There shouldn't be a budgeting problem with things going so well."

"The scheduling needs work," Mayer insisted. He continued to scroll his screen with a pasty index finger.

"We have two full-time and two part-time employees, and we need another full," McKenzie explained, her patience waning as heat seeped into her spine. She wasn't sure if it was anger or fear, but she was flooded with an emotion she hadn't felt in a long time.

Mayer gave her a toothy smile that looked practiced. "There's no need to worry, Miss Price. I'll take it from here." He set the tablet neatly on the table, which she realized had been cleared off and decorated with a phone charger and stapler. "There will be no need for another full-time employee with me here to manage things for my great-uncle. In fact, hours can be reduced."

McKenzie's throat went dry. "So Mr. Hill is your—"

Mayer smiled. "He's stepping back." He looked past McKenzie to the kitchen, and shuddered as if it was an unpleasant sight. "It's not quite what I'm used to, since I've managed grocery chains for over a decade, but with my grandma passing and leaving me her home on Pebble Stretch Road, it seemed the best use of my…inheritance." He smiled again. "Charming town. A little behind the times, but…"

McKenzie clamped her lips together to keep from gagging. Mayer made a pointed examination of his space-age watch. "You are two minutes late clocking in, Miss Price. Scurry, scurry!" The corners of his mouth lifted as if he'd said something funny, but his eyes remained as lifeless as a mackerel's.

She bit back a surge of bile. "So Mr. Hill is not selling the diner at all?"

"'Selling'? With all of the money it's making in this economy? Not right now. It's become quite the hot spot, and online reviews are glowing." Mayer motioned toward the door— a subtle cue for her to leave. "Why would he sell a place doing so well? Especially when he has someone like me that can make it perform even better." He grinned at her, and McKenzie sidestepped her way out of the room and fled to the restroom, fighting a balloon in her chest that was threatening to burst. The diner was not going up for sale? What on earth was Mr.

Hill thinking, bringing a relative in from out of town who knew nothing about how she'd been supervising the diner these past few years?

Ben fought a nagging headache for two days before he finally dug through the medical-supply closet for aspirin. At least the peace and quiet of the office soothed his nerves as he studied the scheduled appointments for the day with the pills in his grip. It was odd not to have the usual surge of adrenaline he was used to feeling when he rushed into work to start a new day. Instead, he'd driven the back country roads of his hometown to drop off Megan at school, appreciating a majestic, corn husk–yellow sunrise. His daughter had stopped complaining to her grandmother that she wanted her to drive in the mornings and quietly accepted that her father would play chauffeur for now. That was progress. Ben wasn't sure how much he should expect from a six-year-old who only saw him occasionally, but Megan seemed to be warming up. After her first dance class, she'd surprised him by talking about the dance studio the entire way home. It had cheered him up, but it didn't erase the discomfort of hearing the song the band had played right before he told McKenzie everything and ruined their friendship.

During their argument in the parking lot afterward, she'd sworn to him there was no way she would leave Kudzu Creek for a loud, crowded city with no family or friends. She didn't care about the arts, dining, culture or the education she could get if she just stepped outside her comfort zone. Ben frowned and chased down the aspirin with a cup of water. Unfortunately, the dance-class song had brought back the one thing he was determined to pretend had never happened.

Ben rubbed his head and leaned back. The appointment-filled day was a welcome distraction. He'd be able to talk to people who needed his expertise—people who actually respected him for what he'd done with his life. He hoped Bailey Roberts would not have an emergency today. He needed a little more time before facing McKenzie again, because at some point, they'd have to tackle what they'd avoided talking about for the past twelve years. Unless she wanted to pretend he'd never offered his heart to her on a platter. He thumbed through the files. It'd been a mistake. He should have never come on so strong back then. It could never happen again, and it wouldn't. He was over her. And he had little Megs to prove it.

Darlene popped inside the door, her black hair

curled and lips brightened with a purplish lip-stick that complemented her dark skin. "Good morning, Young Cooper," she sang, waving a file. "Your first patient is here this morning."

Ben checked the clock. "She's early."

"Honey, Ms. Olivia is always on time, so if she's here, you're late." Darlene grinned, show-ing her bright, square teeth. "Just ask her."

Ben chuckled. Ms. Olivia had taught elemen-tary school when he was a little boy, and even then she'd seemed antiquated, but now she was a walking legend. He pushed his concerns to the back of his mind, slid into his white coat and threw the stethoscope around his neck. After he tapped on the door to room Number One with his knuckles, a voice croaked, "Come in," and he eased inside, shutting the door be-hind him.

"Good morning, Ms. Olivia. How are you this morning?"

"I've been better," she declared as he glanced down at Darlene's notes on the chart. "Your father told me you'd be filling in. How many years young are you, Bentley Cooper?"

Ben smiled. "The big three-oh this year."

She beamed. "And a doctor already? You're still a lad."

"I'm smarter than I look," Ben assured her. "I'm waiting on a surgical fellowship, too."

"A surgeon, huh?"

"Yes, ma'am."

"Well, I need a rocket scientist," Ms. Olivia complained. "I can't work the new blood pressure machine your father gave me. It's too confusing with all those buttons and pictures."

"Did your neighbor show you how to use it?"

"Bradley?" Ms. Olivia nodded, and her hair fell over her eyebrows. Ben realized it wasn't her own. No wonder it looked so unusual. "Oh, yes, several times, and even Claire tried to explain it." Ms. Olivia cocked her head at him, pale eyes brightening. "You know Claire Ainsworth, don't you?"

"I don't believe so." Ben's mind fished backward for a Claire in his past.

Ms. Olivia sniffed. "Oh, you wouldn't. You went to the county high school."

"I did," he said, trying not to sound curt. Kudzu Creek's little high school had grown since he left town, but his parents had allowed him to go to the other option in the county with McKenzie.

"Yes, well, Claire was one of Miss Henny's fosters, and she inherited that great old house. They live there now—her and Bradley."

"I remember Bradley," offered Ben. He was the cousin of Donovan Ainsworth, the high school class president the year Ben had graduated.

"Were you friends?"

"No, not really. I just remember them hanging out whenever Bradley visited." Ben left it at that. There was no need to explain that he hadn't bothered making friends, since people like Scotty and Billy made it difficult.

Ms. Olivia sighed. "Bradley tried to teach me how to use the machine, but I don't understand it." She pouted. "I just plain don't like it. Anything that takes foreign batteries is not to be trusted."

"They're just an unusual size." Ben seated her on the paper-covered examination table and used the old blood pressure machine on the wall as he continued asking questions. A lightheadedness she admitted to him worried him. "Have you fallen?"

"Not any more than usual."

He breathed in with concern. "Do you live alone?"

"Why, no—there's Snoopy and Linus."

Ben wondered if she was as sharp as he'd first assumed. "The *Peanuts* gang?"

"My cat."

"Snoopy is a cat?"

"Why, of course he's a cat. I can't very well have dogs, can I?"

"I'm not sure." Amusement bubbled in Ben's throat. This was very different from the emergency room at Chicago General. "When do you get dizzy?" he probed, and when she answered, he suggested that she drink more water and take her time getting up to move around.

Ms. Olivia wagged her head at the suggestions. "At my age, I don't have a lot of time left, so why slow down now?"

Ben grinned at her attempt to tease him. "Because your body is telling you to. You need to take it easy."

"But the doctors all say to walk and get exercise—even your daddy."

"Maybe with a friend. How about a hobby? Have you thought of that?"

"I have plenty of those." Ms. Olivia ticked off a few committee boards she was on and listed the local book club as well.

"Kudzu Creek has a book club?" Ben said with interest.

"Yes, it's a good bit of fun. We meet at the dining room of the Azalea Inn once a month."

"That sounds nice." Ben pictured a group of old ladies around a tea table, discussing Agatha Christie mysteries. McKenzie's bookstore would have been the perfect spot for a book club, if she'd stuck to it. "I bet you like crime stories," Ben guessed politely.

"Why, yes, I do," Ms. Olivia declared. She reached for an alligator-hide handbag. "Women my age have to stay on top of things like that." Ben helped her up, bending low to hold on to her elbow. "But we read all kinds of stories," she continued. "This month it's a French historical because McKenzie Price likes history, so we always go back in time for her picks."

"McKenzie is in the Kudzu Creek book club?"

"Oh, yes, she's a wonderful girl." Ms. Oliva narrowed her eyes and studied him. "How do you know, Mac?"

"Oh," Ben stammered, "she went to the county high school, too. We were…friends."

"Were you, now?" Ms. Olivia spoke a little more slowly, as if an idea had formed in her mind. "You aren't married anymore, are you?" Ben felt his cheeks warm. "Your momma told me awhile back when the baby came." She pointed an accusing finger at him. "I haven't forgotten you didn't invite me to the wedding."

"It was across the country." Ben coughed.

"Hm," said Ms. Olivia. "Well, McKenzie works just down the street at Southern Fried

Kudzu." Ms. Olivia proceeded to point in the diner's general direction. "*Lovely* girl," she said, emphasizing *lovely*. She grinned at Ben with all the innocence of a Vegas card shark. "Did you know she's still single?" Ben choked on a reply and found himself hurrying her to the door. "Never found 'the one,'" Ms. Olivia said with a dramatic sigh, and Ben imagined she'd probably make air quotes with her fingers if she knew how.

"Is that so?" He guided her down the hall and past Darlene, who was smiling over some paperwork, which meant she was listening to every word.

"Oh, yes." Ms. Olivia sighed once more as if McKenzie's relationship status were a Greek tragedy. "She keeps to herself, takes care of her sister and won't settle because..."

"She's a hard worker," Ben supplied.

"The smart ones never settle, Ms. Olivia," agreed Darlene, standing to reach for the file tucked under Ben's arm. He forced a smile in response, wondering what these elegant magnolias thought of his brief marriage, which had produced a child being raised by his parents. His chest tightened, but he managed to say, "Goodbye, now," To Ms. Olivia after suggesting she visit the Knight's Pharmacy blood pressure machine on the days she couldn't manage her new contraption. When he hurried back down the hall to grab the next file, he passed a framed picture of his parents and Megan when she was two. It looked odd to see the three of them without him—and without Megan's mother, Chetana. A fragmented family unit with two vital members missing.

His heart pinched. If he had patients in Chicago like his father did here, he'd probably smile as much as he did. Maybe he'd still be married. Ms. Olivia's conversation left him in a light mood—not with the desperate and depressed feelings he experienced after some of the violent cases he dealt with from the city streets. But he was a little sad, too. He'd wanted a family of his own and yet had failed miserably at that. He was nothing like his father.

Ben pushed open the next patient's door with a glance at the file in his hand. A Mr. Dougherty was planted on the stool beside the examination table, in overalls and rubber slide-on shoes. His eyes followed him into the room, glossy with suspicion. "Who're you?"

"I'm Dr. Cooper."

"You're not Dr. Cooper," argued the old farmer. His face looked unnaturally ruddy, and Ben wondered if this was another blood pressure problem. "I know Dr. Cooper. I've been his patient for over twenty-five years."

Ben smiled and hoped it looked friendly. "I'm his son, Ben." He caught himself. "I mean, Dr. Bentley Cooper. I'll be filling in for the next few months until he's recovered from heart surgery."

"Oh yeah," grumbled the old man. He crossed his arms and leaned back on the rotating stool meant for the doctor. "Bentley. Like the car. Fancy automobile." He maneuvered a toothpick from one side of his mouth to the other, examining Ben's wristwatch. "Old Doc Cooper's boy. Ain't you been in New York?"

"Chicago," Ben corrected him, looking at his clipboard.

"So?" grunted the old man. He heaved himself off the stool. "I don't need no city doctor that don't know me."

"I assure you, I'm just as capable as my father."

"Son, you aren't from around here," the farmer informed Ben. "I don't know you, and you don't know me. And the only medicine I trust is your daddy's, so you have him call me when he gets to feeling better."

"But—"

"This ain't a conversation," Mr. Dougherty cut in. "I'm telling you how it's going to be."

With that, the old man lumbered out of the room, leaving Ben with his mouth agape. Annoyance erupted from out of nowhere, and he dropped the clipboard down on the empty examination table with a sharp exhale. The patient had come in for a follow-up, and by his flushed face and heavy breathing, he obviously needed to be checked out. Ben's nerves vibrated with frustration. It was going to be a long week, and he had nothing to no cases to take home to discuss with his dad. Not to mention there was his daughter who didn't seem to care if he left town again.

Chapter Five

McKenzie dropped Bailey off at school, took the new inhaler in to the school nurse and then hurried to Southern Fried Kudzu. Mr. Mayer was rigid about being on time, and she wanted to make sure she was five minutes early. The past few days had been tense, with Barney sending her looks of confusion as if an alien spaceship had landed on the roof. The manager had made him refry a few hamburgers he deemed less than perfect, which backed up the tickets, which in turn backed up the line, causing McKenzie to spend most of her time assuring everyone she would get to them. There was also a change from carrying meals to the table to calling out the customers' receipt numbers when the food was ready. The new system made her feel like she was at a truck stop, shouting off lotto numbers. Lastly, the new time card routine required her to log into it on her phone while moving around the back, trying to get a good signal. It was like attempting to clock in to another century without the rocket fuel she needed.

Tossing her jacket onto the same hook she'd used for years, McKenzie skipped around for a phone signal by waving her arms, then hurried to the kitchen to start the fruit tarts after finally logging in. To her shock, Mayer was in the kitchen at her counter, rolling out a thin dough. "Oh," she said in surprise.

"Many hands make light work," he informed her.

McKenzie wanted to point out she made the dry mix weekly, and it took a special touch. Besides, she'd been making the desserts since her second year at the diner. Everyone in town knew she made the tarts in the pastry case. "Do you want me to take over?"

"No, Miss Price. I can follow a recipe," Mayer responded in his cut-and-dry tone.

"Where's the green-and-brown ceramic mixing bowl?"

"That old thing?" He winced. "It had a crack. Not very sanitary, you know. This new one will be more efficient, and it looks more professional."

McKenzie glanced at the large stainless steel bowl on the counter. He was right—but this was a diner in Kudzu Creek, not a bakery in downtown Atlanta. "That looks like quite a bit of dough."

"Daily batches aren't going to cut it in a fast-paced environment," Mayer admonished her. "We have a catering delivery today, too. Why don't you start the coffee?"

The firm suggestion stung. "Are you sure?"

"Yes, I'll make enough tarts for the weekend."

"They might get a little stale," McKenzie warned.

"Not if we wrap them up and put them in the freezer."

McKenzie felt concern knot in her chest. "Then we'll have to thaw them out. They'll get a little gooey. Taste different."

"Now, Miss Price, I know I'm not a pastry chef," Mayer chided her, "but neither are you. This is a family recipe, isn't it? That's all people care about. Now, scurry. The coffee machines are waiting, and you can unlock the front of the store. People like to see your face."

McKenzie marched woodenly to the front

door. There was still a half hour until opening, and flipping the sign would invite people
in too early before the food was ready. She reminded herself it was Wednesday. That meant
she was halfway through the week, and Mayer
had said she would be the one to deliver lunch
to the health clinic. McKenzie liked the idea of
escaping for a few minutes, but she told herself it had nothing to do with Ben. Her stomach
fluttered, until she looked over her shoulder at
the coffee machine, hoping the hot beverage
had already started. Beside it was a new, enormous, shiny machine. *Lattes?* She groaned, unlocked the door and hurried to the counter to
start the coffee.

True, some of the younger set might enjoy a
latte, but the majority of their customers came
in for a brew Mr. Hill had been ordering from
Colombia for over fifty years. There was also
raw cacao because not everyone drank coffee.
McKenzie reached for the bag of grounds under
the counter and pulled out a new brand of coffee in different packaging. It'd been cultivated
by a giant food company and was of a much
cheaper quality. And the bag of cacao was nowhere in sight. Biting her lip to keep from tear-
ing up, McKenzie poured the cheap coffee into
the machine without changing the filter. Her

throat tightened. Why was she crying over coffee? The Hills had decided to keep the diner a little longer, and they wanted to make sure it ran the best it could .

Suddenly, McKenzie's years of sacrifice and hard work seemed unappreciated. Thin tears tumbled over her bottom lashes, and she hurried to the bathroom, grabbing a bottle of cleaner on the way as if she intended to do some scrubbing. Never mind the fact that it had probably been done the night before. She laid a wet towel over her face and took a deep breath. It was just a little change. Ben drifted back into her thoughts. Maybe Mr. Mayer, like Ben, would only be here a little while. He'd leave soon, like most newcomers did, and she'd return things to normal. She just had to hang on a little longer, and the diner would be hers. McKenzie collected herself, nearly slipping on a piece of toilet paper when she started to leave. It was then she realized the bathroom had not been cleaned after closing the night before— so she gave it a good once-over and made sure it was done right. Mayer may not have needed her, but the diner did.

Ben's stomach rumbled, and he hurried to the office to dig through the desk drawer for a mint to hold himself over. He hadn't packed a lunch because of Darlene's reminder that meals were catered by Southern Fried Kudzu every other Wednesday. With his mind on McKenzie, who he expected was at the diner, he skimmed through the morning's cases. Mrs. Chester didn't have strep throat but a sinus infection; the Ball siblings needed testing for dairy allergies; and Mr. Wagoner had shown up, complaining of joint pain. Ben had recommended he see a physical therapist, along with his usual injections. Three patients had canceled—two old-timers and a name he didn't recognize. It had seemed they didn't want to have a new doctor. It felt like a punch to the chest every time someone balked at seeing him, but Ben tried not to take it personally. When the clock read an hour after noon, he inhaled something that smelled delicious, and his mouth watered. Striding to the front office, he discovered Darlene and Mindy holding paper cups of iced tea in their hands. They each had small salads and were opening their utensil packets. "Is our meal here?"

"McKenzie's just setting up." Darlene hooked a flaming-red thumbnail toward the small room behind the fax machine.

McKenzie? Ben hadn't expected her to deliver the catered meal. He'd tried not to dwell on her *too* much. The patients who'd appreciated him, along with the ones who'd rejected him for not being his father, were almost enough of a distraction. Ben opened the door to the break room and found her setting up foil trays on a little table. The air smelled sweet and sour, and her silhouette made his heart leap back in time as if they were kids again. She moved quietly and efficiently with her hair up, showing off chocolate-brown tendrils that curled at the nape of her neck. She'd been his morning star for so long, and here she was after all these years, still shining. He caught himself. The old scars on his heart sternly reined in the memories. The diner? A bookstore? Freedom? Sanctuary? He didn't know what she wanted anymore. "I didn't know you made deliveries."

She jumped as if caught with her hand in the cookie jar. "I was just about finished."

She didn't want to see him, Ben realized. Was it because of the memories sparked by the song at the kids' dance class? He tried not to look bothered by that. "Business must be as good as they say."

McKenzie wiped a loose lock of hair that had fallen out of her ponytail. "Yes, and we're a little shorthanded."

"So you do the deliveries now?"

"We have a new manager."

Ben walked over to examine the offerings, and his stomach rumbled at the fried rice and sautéed vegetables, which included chunks of pineapples beside the side salads.

"This is what your dad usually orders from us," McKenzie explained.

"Yes, he told me about the catering."

"It's very generous."

"I'm starved."

McKenzie smiled. "Help yourself." She motioned at a paper plate. "Should I call in Darlene and Mindy? I gave them their drinks and salads."

"They'll be in shortly." Against all of his heart's admonitions, Ben wished for a few minutes alone with her, even though she was acting like she wanted to escape. He picked up a plate and tapped it on his leg. "I thought you managed Southern Fried Kudzu?"

"Not officially. I was the supervisor." McKenzie's voice sounded strained. She wouldn't meet his eyes.

"My mom said she heard from Mrs. Hill they're selling soon?"

"Not anymore. It's doing so well they decided to hold on to it a little longer."

Ben raised his brows with curiosity. "And they hired a new manager."

With rosy cheeks, McKenzie sank into a nearby chair. "I asked for more help."

"That was good of you to be transparent," Ben began, trying to sound positive.

"But I didn't mean for…"

"New management."

"Yeah." McKenzie sighed. She crossed one leg over the other. "The truth is, I was hoping to buy it soon, but I'm not sure how long that'll take now."

"So you'll have to work there a little longer."

"Yes, Ben, I will." Her tone sounded sharp.

"I'm sorry. I didn't mean to—"

"Never mind." McKenzie rose and started crumpling paper bags. "I'm sorry. It's not you. I'm just used to doing things my way, and now I have to wait again to have a business. I thought it'd happen this year, in time for Christmas, but so much for hopes and wishes."

Ben began loading his plate. "I noticed the town still doesn't have a bookstore."

"We have the library."

He pointed at McKenzie with a ladle. "That's not a bookstore." When her jaw tightened, he concentrated on the juicy pineapple so he wouldn't have to acknowledge her offense.

"That's not a hangout spot with lounge chairs and pastries and the smell of coffee."

"The diner's close enough," she said with little enthusiasm.

He glanced back. "But wasn't that the dream?"

"The dream changed."

Ben didn't believe her. He wanted to push her, to make her admit that maybe she never believed in the dream at all. "Ms. Olivia told me you run the local book club."

McKenzie gave a small chuckle of surprise. "I don't," she explained. "It's Ms. Diane's baby— you know, the owner next door at Alabaster's?" Ben shook his head. "She has a couple kids younger than us. Did you know Beau Morris?"

"I'm not sure. What high school?"

McKenzie lifted her chin as if remembering the two different high schools in the area. "City school. So no, you wouldn't have. Diane opened Alabaster's a few years ago, and we've become good friends. Since she's next door, she's a regular in the mornings."

"That's nice." Ben reached for a set of plastic cutlery.

"Ben?"

He looked back.

"What was that with Scotty and Billy last week?"

"Nothing." Ben pulled out a chair and tried to act indifferent, but she'd known him too long to be fooled, even if it had been forever since they'd seen one another.

McKenzie stared. "Are you sure?"

He was tempted to take a bite to fill his mouth, but he set down his fork and pulled in a deep breath instead. "It wasn't anything different than usual," he said, hoping he sounded indifferent. "They wanted to know what I was doing there and when I was leaving."

"I'm sure they didn't mean it that way," McKenzie said haltingly.

He raised his brows.

"Oh, okay," she muttered. "Yes, they made a few remarks after you left. Some people don't change. It's a sad fact of life."

He shrugged. "There are patients who won't even come into the clinic with my dad not there."

McKenzie leaned forward and touched his arm. The brush of her fingers warmed him all the way to his bones. "Don't let that bother you, Ben. You're still helping people that need you. People like Scotty and Billy are jealous. They always have been. You're smart, and you went off and did great things with your talents. They're just reliving their glory days."

"Yes. I know you're right, and I'm fine now."

McKenzie fell silent. Ben turned back to his plate. *This is good,* he thought. Airing out the past was therapeutic. There was just one thing left to discuss: The band concert. The big question. And her driving away and never speaking to him again until he'd rolled back into town this year. The door pushed open wide, and Darlene and Mindy strolled in. Darlene sighed. "Smells delicious!"

"I should get back to work," said McKenzie.

"Me too." But Ben didn't want her to go. He wanted her to stay so he could explain everything. He fiddled with his plate until Darlene and Mindy left with their food. "You know I was married, right?" he blurted out

McKenzie stopped gathering her things and froze. "Yes, but not her name."

"Chetana." Ben gulped. "She was from New York. I'm sorry about… We just invited immediate family to the ceremony. It happened fast."

McKenzie shrugged. "It's fine. I saw it in the newspaper."

"I'm sorry, anyway. I know a lot of people around here felt left out. Ms. Olivia even mentioned it."

McKenzie chuckled. "She does like to keep tabs."

"I know." Ben took a deep breath. "I know Chicago is far away. Chetana was—*is*—well…" he stammered, sinking into McKenzie's forget-me-not-blue-eyed gaze he'd never forgotten. "We're the same but different—very different. I'm from here, and she's from the East Coast. We came from two different worlds but were so much alike in our ambitions we thought—well, *I* thought—I'd have a partner by my side who loved what I loved and that we could make it work, but it became one big competition."

"She's a doctor, too?"

Ben nodded. "I tried to make it last," he assured McKenzie, "but she didn't want a child, and we couldn't come to an agreement about that. I gave in and asked her to marry me anyway."

"So you have custody?"

"Yes. I was happy when Megan came along. Chetana was not. She surrendered her to me and only asks for visitation one week in the summer."

"Wow." McKenzie frowned, and Ben's heart sank, knowing she must have been thinking about her mother.

"She was born to be a doctor and nothing but a doctor. Like me."

McKenzie studied him. "We're born to do a

lot of things, but I don't think they're meant to be exclusive or more important than family."

Ben suddenly felt stricken.

"That's not all you were born for," McKenzie continued. "You're a good son. I'm sure you're trying to be a good father, too."

Her assessment made his stomach roll over, and he pushed his plate away. "Not good enough. You saw Megan last week. She treats me like I'm just a visitor in her life. I guess that's all I have been."

"It's because she knows you're not staying. That it's just temporary. But it doesn't have to be, Ben. You could come home. She needs you."

Ben clasped his hands on top of the table. "I can't. Not right now. But I want you to know that I'm not a terrible person. I had to finish my residency. I didn't want her in childcare in some strange city, and Mom pleaded with me to let her take her for the time being."

"And Chetana's family?"

He shook his head. "I think Chetana was running away from herself. Her family never accepted me, and they aren't interested in seeing Megan. I don't even know how much they know about her."

"That's awful. I'm so sorry. Maybe they'll

come around in time." McKenzie's eyes pooled with tears.

"I'm sorry. I don't mean to dredge up any pain for you."

She shook her head. "You haven't."

"How are your parents?"

"Dad's in Florida with Freida. He married her three years ago after Marlene." McKenzie sat back and crossed her arms.

"Marlene?" Ben squinted, trying to remember.

"He married Marlene after you went away. They moved to Florida not long afterward."

"And you didn't go?"

"He didn't want me to go with them," McKenzie said in a casual tone.

Ben shook his head in disbelief, and she raised a hand to staunch his pity. "It's not like I wanted to go. Besides, these days I have the diner… Jill—" She stopped abruptly. "You know my sister's husband died."

He nodded. "I heard about it. I'm sorry."

"She needed me until she met Tim, and I never wanted to leave home anyway. This town is part of me."

"Yes," said Ben dryly, "I remember that."

McKenzie looked down; maybe he'd gone too far.

"Look," Ben continued in a rush, "about last Friday—" He took a deep breath that pinched the muscles in his chest. "I didn't mean to dash out of the dance studio. I'm sorry about that and about everything that happened back then."

"Don't," McKenzie interjected, her face flushed. "It's okay." She reached out and rested her slender fingers over his.

"I just want you to know I'm sorry things ended the way they did."

"Me too." McKenzie gave him a faint smile. "We can still be friends, right? Just like old times?"

For some reason, her offer of surrender made Ben's heart sink a little instead of buoying him. "Sure," he replied, feeling a sheet of detachment drape over him. *Friends. Just like old times.* At least he knew now not to do anything to mess it up a second time. If he was ever unlucky enough to have feelings for McKenzie Price again, he knew he'd best keep them to himself.

Chapter Six

McKenzie was surprised to find her shift shortened by two hours on Friday, but with a spark of enthusiasm, she realized she'd be able to take Bailey to dance lessons again. Part of her was rather eager to see Ben. She'd enjoyed their time together when she took the food order to the clinic. The senior Dr. Cooper's nurse and secretary seemed to adore Ben, and McKenzie liked seeing him in a white coat there, even with his silly car behind the building. She wondered if she could ever convince him he didn't need a fancy car for people to respect him—but then again, he'd never had one of his own in high school. Dr. Cooper was a practical man. He'd encouraged his son to get a job and save money for his own wheels, but Ben wouldn't sacrifice the study time he'd needed to conquer his advanced classes. He'd been the salutatorian of their graduating class, but that hadn't been enough. Back then, one critical remark would set him back for days. Teasing had made him a servant to ambition. McKenzie released a breath of hopelessness. All the respect in the world didn't seem like it would ever be enough for Ben. He clearly had no intentions of staying in Kudzu Creek, even for Megan's sake.

"Bailey? Are you ready?" she called out from the kitchen. The little girl hurried to the car, and they made it to Miss Sherry's studio five minutes early. McKenzie noted Ben's car in the lot—parked on the side so it wouldn't be dinged. She shook her head and followed Bailey inside, where Megan spotted her and grinned. McKenzie waved at her.

"Hi, Miss McKenzie," said the little girl. "I'm practicing my cartwheels."

"That's wonderful," McKenzie replied. "I'm sure you'll get it in no time."

She found Ben in the corner of the room, watching the chaos. The Ainsworth twins were running in circles, tapping each girl on the head with too much gusto. Bailey ordered the two boys to calm down, and Claire Ainsworth's daughter jumped up and began to chase her twin cousins around the room. Claire waved. "Hello, there. It's good to see you."

McKenzie smiled. "You too. How's Bradley?"

"Working late on a reno job again, but we're fine." She waved a book in her hand. "I'm trying to finish the book you suggested."

"Are you liking it?"

Claire nodded.

McKenzie smiled with satisfaction and plopped down beside Ben to talk. "You're playing chauffeur again, I see."

"I wondered if I'd see you here again," he admitted. He didn't seem to mind, and for some reason, this made McKenzie more than a little pleased.

"Jill had to work. The factory changed her shift a few weeks ago," she explained.

Ben wrenched his lips. "Not everyone's understanding when it comes to single parents." He hesitated as if he'd never applied the observation to himself. "I heard they're going to learn the cha-cha today."

"That should be interesting." McKenzie grinned. "Remember when we partnered up for it in gym class in middle school?"

Ben groaned. "Gosh, I was so uncoordinated," he moaned. "No wonder everyone made fun of me. Sorry if I ruined your toes for life."

McKenzie extended her boots out in front of her. "They're still there," she joked. "Although some days I wonder how long my arches will hold out."

Miss Sherry's flamboyant arrival commanded everyone's attention when she traipsed into the room, wearing a white-and-black dress with a pink scarf. "Who's ready to cha-cha today?"

"Not me," shouted Leo Ainsworth above the din of excited little girls.

McKenzie burst into giggles. Ben laughed—and for a second, he seemed like the old Ben, not Dr. Bentley Cooper. McKenzie followed his gaze and saw him studying Megan. She sought out Bailey again, and McKenzie realized just how close the two girls were becoming as Michael Bublé's "Sway" began to drift through the overhead speakers. The class began mimicking Miss Sherry's footwork. McKenzie hummed under her breath, and to her surprise, Ben began to sing softly. Megan and Bailey giggled as they stepped forward and back, side by side, with Megan picking up the steps quickly.

"She's really good," McKenzie observed. "She has rhythm."

"She doesn't get it from me," Ben joked.

McKenzie looked away, concentrating on

the class's enthusiasm as her senior prom surfaced in her memories. She hadn't made it, and that was her fault, she realized. She sighed inwardly as a twinge of regret made her wonder what it would have been like if she'd gone with Ben. Her friends had told her how the old warehouse in town—now the library—was decorated beautifully and how much fun it'd been, but she assured them she'd made plenty of tips working to make missing the dance worth it.

Had it been? She chewed her bottom lip as Miss Sherry began lining up the class in two rows facing one another. McKenzie had earned a degree, but what had she done with it? Nothing yet—and with Mayer around, who knew how long it'd be before Mr. Hill decided to sell the diner.

"All right, class, now we are going to partner up." Miss Sherry looked around the room, and her gaze stopped on McKenzie. "Let's use a couple moms and dads to show you." She pointed at McKenzie and Ben.

McKenzie's eyes widened. "Oh, no, I can't."

"Sure you can," Miss Sherry insisted. "Come on up, McKenzie, and bring Dr. Cooper with you."

Beside her, Ben stiffened. "I can't dance," he said.

McKenzie nodded. "He can't, trust me." The other parents around them tittered, and Ben gave McKenzie a look of indignation. Ignoring him, she continued, "Besides, I'm an aunt, not a parent."

"Aunts count," Miss Sherry decreed, then turned her vivid stare on Ben. "And it sounds like it's time for you to learn."

The children burst into giggles. "Come on, Aunt McKenzie!" cheered Bailey. "Do it!"

McKenzie pursed her lips and noticed Megan watching her father with round eyes. She thought she saw a spark of hopeful interest. McKenzie grabbed Ben by the arm and dragged him to his feet with determination. "Come on, Bentley Boy. Let's show them how it's done."

"But I—"

"Your daughter's watching," McKenzie whispered. The parents began to clap, Claire hooted, and McKenzie gave them all a gratuitous wave as she joined the children on the dance floor in front of their teacher. Ben's face turned a shade of plum, and when she reached for his hands, they were hot. His fingers curled around hers, and any bemusement she felt faded as a light current shot up to her elbows. Her heart stumbled. Why was she putting him under the spotlight like he'd once done to her?

Ben surrendered with a shuddering wince as they began to move robotically at Miss Sherry's command. After a few notes, his stiff movements became natural, and McKenzie began to enjoy herself. She smiled at him. He quirked his lips in return—and suddenly, it was as if they had been dancing together for years, picking up the steps they'd learned in gym class as kids. He grabbed her other hand and spun her across the floor with silly, galloping cha-cha steps that made the children *ooh*, and Miss Sherry put her hands on her hips. "That is not a part of the routine!" she called out.

McKenzie threw back her head and laughed, then gave a flourished little wiggle as they reached the wall. She caught Ben's eyes in the mirror, and he erupted into gales of laughter that she hadn't realized she'd missed. He mimicked her wiggle, and they both bowed to the class as the children broke out in thunderous applause.

Miss Sherry shushed the room. "All right, all right, I think we have the general idea," she admitted, giving McKenzie and Ben a dramatic eye roll. She pointed toward the bleachers. "You two show-offs take a seat." Chuckling, Ben led McKenzie to the bench, where the other parents congratulated them. McKenzie thanked everyone as Ben dropped her hand from his grip. She was reluctant to let go because, oddly, it felt right. She brushed a loose lock of hair behind her ear, noticing how flushed she looked in the mirror across the room. Claire met McKenzie's eyes with a grin, then leaned forward and tapped Ben on the shoulder. "Is that your daughter?"

"Her name is Megan."

"She's beautiful."

"Thank you."

"You're a doctor," Claire continued, as if needing to check her facts.

The carefree smile faded. Ben composed himself as if he'd been acting silly for too long. "Why, yes, I'm Dr. Bentley Cooper. I'm filling in at the clinic while my father recovers from surgery."

"How wonderful. That's good to know," Claire chirped. She turned to McKenzie. "And he dances, too!"

"Yes, the dancing doctor," responded McKenzie airily. Claire chuckled. McKenzie hadn't meant to sound witty, because she certainly wasn't feeling that way. Ben had pulled back on his virtual white coat as if they had not just danced together around the room and made everyone laugh. She searched for Megan and saw the little girl concentrating on her footwork, but every few seconds, she glanced up to examine her father as if she'd never seen him before. McKenzie put a hand to her chest to ease her beating heart. She wondered if it was from exertion or her dance partner. Her face wrinkled in puzzlement, and she caught her reaction in the mirror. Her eyes were bright; cheeks glowing. McKenzie inhaled quietly and averted her gaze. She wasn't sure she recognized Ben at that moment, and she certainly didn't recognize herself.

Ben felt like he was walking on rainbows. Megan loved her dance lesson late Friday afternoon, and on Saturday she'd allowed him to follow her around while she fed the animals and collected chicken eggs without any looks of suspicion. She'd even hurried to him when he called her over to show her an owl in one of the pine trees. Ben had assured her that screech owls rarely bothered chickens, although he warned her to keep an eye on any new chicks. She'd given a solemn nod and then returned to her duties. On Sunday, he invited her to ride with him to church, and when she looked back and forth between him and her grandmother, Mom suggested that they all ride together. This seemed to please the little girl best.

The three arrived at Grace Chapel downtown just five minutes before the sermon began. It was the first time Ben felt collected and comfortable enough to greet all the old familiar faces at church. Mom hurried them along inside, holding Megan's hand, and Ben followed as they entered the crowded sanctuary. He looked for McKenzie, as he used to do in the past, and found her in the next-to-last row, seated beside her sister. Bailey was between them and didn't miss a beat. "Over here, Megan!" she called out in a loud whisper that could be heard all the way to the pulpit. A few heads turned. Ben caught McKenzie's eye, and she motioned to the space beside her. Ben tapped his mother on the shoulder and pointed.

"There's a spot."

"Oh, okay," murmured his mother. "I'm so glad you and McKenzie are friends again."

Ben flushed at her searching glance but led the way without another word, sitting beside McKenzie while Megan scooted past him to get to Bailey. When Mom sat down on his other side, Ben was pressed closer to McKenzie. He shrugged helplessly, and she made a noise of amusement in her throat.

He settled in, feeling himself relax as he inhaled the familiar scents of his childhood:

polished pews, floral soap and the indescribable sensation of peace that made his heart feel like warm maple syrup. His shoulder touched McKenzie's, and a familiar sensation of connection, companionship and something else washed over him. He snuck a look at her profile. Her shoulder-length hair was down, and a long gold chain looped across the neckline of her sweater. She'd put on a little makeup around her blue eyes, which made them stand out, and her lips had a slight sheen that made them look like satin.

Ben jerked his attention back to the pulpit with a start. He had no business thinking about her that way. After all this time, she'd finally accepted his friendship again, and it wasn't fair for him to ruin that for her. She was a wonderful friend, and that was all she'd ever be. When the service was over, he rose to his feet as if to stretch, anxious to put more space between himself and the woman beside him. She stood and smiled.

"How're your toes?"

"Fine. Yours?" asked Ben.

"You didn't do any damage. I think you might have improved."

He laughed in disbelief. "Really?"

"You're a good dancer, Dr. Cooper," Bailey chimed in.

Ben looked down and saw Megan brighten at her friend's approval. "I'm not sure Miss Sherry thinks so, but thank you, Bailey." He caught himself almost crouching to her level as memories of his pediatric rotation raced through his mind. He'd enjoyed it, but pediatrics wasn't a surgery career in a prestigious hospital. "How are you feeling?"

"Okay." She looked at her mother and aunt. "We've been practicing the cha-cha at home, and I don't need my inhaler."

"I'm glad to hear that." Ben glanced at McKenzie.

She nodded. "Yes, she's had a good week. It just seems to be when she's outdoors."

"I wonder if it's allergy related," he mused.

"It does get worse in the fall." Jill leaned over and offered a hand. "How are you, Ben? Thanks for taking care of Bailey."

"You're welcome. Have you had her tested?"

"Yes, she was tested for several things when she was a toddler."

"It may be time to do that again."

"Okay." A look of concern crossed over Jill's face. "Do you do that there? At the clinic?

Ben shook his head. "No, but I can give you a referral. Let me talk to my dad."

"Thank you." Jill smiled her appreciation and turned to embrace one of the senior sisters from the congregation who'd tapped her on the shoulder.

"Aunt McKenzie," chimed Bailey. She squeezed past Ben in the pew and pulled on McKenzie's hand. "Can Megan come to our house for a sleepover?"

Ben froze. To his knowledge, Megan had not been invited to many parties. She was quiet and shy, much like he had been, and she'd only stayed with the Prices a couple of times. He held his breath.

"Oh, um…" McKenzie looked at Ben, but he stared back helplessly. He wasn't a mother, and he didn't know what sleepovers were about these days.

He gave his head a hesitant shake. "I don't know…"

McKenzie raised a brow, then turned back to her niece. "Let Dr. Cooper and I talk about it, and we'll get back to you."

"Tonight?"

"No, not tonight."

"How about Friday?" Bailey persisted.

McKenzie glanced at Ben with a hint of a smile. "Maybe—we'll see."

"We'll think about it and let you know," Ben promised.

This seemed to satisfy the girls, but Ben heard Bailey turn to Megan and say, "Friday, okay?" and knew McKenzie and Jill were in for a confrontation later.

"Hello, Doctor," crooned a throaty voice. Ms. Olivia hobbled down the pew in front of him. Following behind her was a group of familiar-looking women.

"Hello, Dr. Cooper. I'm Diane Morris. How's your father?" asked the one with short hair and bright eyes.

"He's doing much better, thank you," replied Ben. "Just not ready to sit for a long spell on wooden pews."

"I can certainly understand that," declared Ms. Olivia.

A man maneuvered through the crowd of ladies and offered a hand. "Dr. Bentley, welcome back to Kudzu Creek."

Ben hesitated to respond, unsure of who he was, although he, too, looked familiar.

"Bradley Ainsworth," he said, touching his chest. He motioned toward one of the other women with Diane and Ms. Oliva. "That's my wife, Claire, who you met at the dance studio, and we have a daughter named Emily. Oh, and I used to spend a lot of weekends here," he added with a smile. "With my cousin, Donovan, under the Friday-night lights."

"That's right," Ben recalled. "I'm surprised you remember me."

"I remember a lot of kids in the band," said Bradley with another friendly smile. "Trumpet, right?"

Ben tried not to wince. "Mellophone, but close enough."

Bradley shook his head with a chuckle. "Music wasn't my forte,' he admitted, "but I admired anyone who could play anything. I respect your father, too."

Ben blinked. No one had ever told him they admired him for being in an orchestra or marching band. But everyone liked his dad.

"We were just asking about his father," said Diane to Bradley. "He's feeling better."

"We convinced him to take a walk yesterday," Ben informed them. He motioned toward Megan. "Or Megan did."

The little girl stopped whispering to Bailey and gazed up at the adults with a meek smile, then scurried away.

Bailey gave chase. "Wait for me!"

"I'm glad to hear that," said Bradley. "Give him our best wishes, won't you?"

Ben bobbed his head in agreement. "It was good to see you."

"You too," Bradley assured him.

"We're glad you're here—aren't we, ladies?" Ms. Olivia piped up. "I got my new prescription, and I'm feeling better than ever."

"You're taking it easy, right?" Ben inquired.

She gave him a mischievous smile. "I can stand up without rocking like a boat, if that's what you mean." From beside Ben, McKenzie let out a soft laugh. "Oh, and don't you forget, McKenzie, we have book club at the end of this month," Ms. Olivia reminded her.

"I won't forget," promised McKenzie. "I'm supposed to lead the discussion."

Ms. Olivia pivoted back to Ben. "You should come, too. Did you read the book?"

"Um, no," he admitted. "You told me about it… Napoleon something?"

"Yes, his romances," crowed Ms. Oliva. Diane laughed.

McKenzie gave Ben's elbow an overt nudge. "Yes, you should come," she repeated in a teasing tone. "It's a little brunch at our friend Lindsey's inn with all of us ladies."

Ben narrowed his eyes, hoping she'd catch the hint that he was trying to beg off.

Spending his lunch break with McKenzie was a tempting idea but not in a room full of women his mother's age. "Perhaps my mom—" Ben began.

"If she can," said Diane kindly, "but we know she runs the food pantry on Wednesday—or that was her reason the last time I asked. Plus, I know she's busy with your dad."

Ben gave her an agreeable smile.

"If you're on a break," insisted McKenzie.

He gave a noncommittal nod.

"Or—" interjected Claire Ainsworth, "you can come to dinner next Tuesday evening." As the other ladies trotted away, she remained behind. She looked at McKenzie. "You promised to come over sometime when Lindsey could make it out. She's free on Tuesday… So why don't you guys come? It'll be a pre-Thanksgiving escape party, with no turkey. Just fun stuff."

"Oh, um…" stammered McKenzie with a sideways glance at Ben. He saw her cheeks take on a bit of color and suddenly felt like they were being tagged as a pair—a couple. Didn't Claire know he and McKenzie were just friends?"

"I wouldn't want to impose," he said coolly.

"You wouldn't be," Claire insisted. "Bradley and I already talked about it. We'd love to have you. Lindsey and Donovan will be there with their twins and new baby. You can bring Megan, and McKenzie can bring Bailey and Jill."

"Are you sure?" Ben tried to look indifferent, but he was flattered to be included in a dinner party with people his age from Kudzu Creek.

"I'm absolutely sure." Claire gave McKenzie a stern stare. "You'll be there, right?"

McKenzie glanced at Ben. "Okay. If you insist."

"I do," said Claire. "I'll let you know as soon as we have a time. It'll be fun to do something before Thanksgiving to take the pressure off everyone."

McKenzie smiled like it was nothing, and Claire waved goodbye. Ben cleared his throat and moved into the center aisle to join the foot traffic trickling out of the sanctuary. He heard McKenzie a few steps behind him as he headed for their car, where he assumed Megan and his mom would be waiting.

"I'm sorry you got roped into my invitation," said McKenzie with a sigh as she caught up beside him.

"Don't be," Ben assured her. He wondered if she was bothered that he'd been invited.

"I know your father wants to spend as much time with you as possible."

That much was true. "It was nice of them— and I'm sure Megan will enjoy it, if you don't mind."

"Of course I don't, and neither will Bailey," said McKenzie. "It'll be fun."

He stopped searching for any weight in her words. It was just a bunch of friends getting together. She obviously wasn't reading anything into it, so he shouldn't, either. "I'll have time. The clinic isn't open that late."

McKenzie gave a faint smile. "I'll be off at the diner, thank goodness."

Ben gave her a casual nod, but his heart hummed with anticipation over spending more time with family and friends instead of patients. But spending too much time with a certain friend… He wasn't sure that was such a good idea. "I guess I should get to know a few people since I hope to come back more often."

McKenzie stopped beside a little compact car he assumed was hers, and he resisted the urge to put his hands in his pockets and linger.

"So when do you think you'll head back to Chicago?" she asked.

"Soon, if my dad is doing okay. I'm off until after Christmas, but I'm hoping to get a fellowship for my specialty, so most likely I'll have to move."

"So you won't be coming back to Kudzu Creek?"

Her words had an edge that he didn't miss. Ben wondered if she'd meant *ever.* "I've sent my résumé out to some other hospitals.

"So you may end up in New York or someplace like that?"

"I don't know," Ben admitted. "Maybe Atlanta." He'd sent an application to Emory, too.

"Oh?" McKenzie looked interested. "Would you live nearby, then? I know it'd be quite a drive."

He stared back but could see nothing behind her eyes. Could he live in Kudzu Creek again— the town that had once made him feel unwelcome and unaccepted? A place where he'd fallen for his best friend, and she'd broken his heart? "I don't know," he said with some hesitance. "It's three hours away. There wouldn't be a reason to…"

McKenzie inhaled sharply. "You do have a daughter. What about Megan?" Her tone sounded accusatory.

Ben stepped back, confused. "She's perfectly fine with my parents."

"Forever?" McKenzie looked across the

parking lot, and he followed her gaze to his little girl, who was waiting beside the car with her grandmother. "Well, at least she gets to see you right now." She exhaled heavily.

Ben cleared his throat. "She does seem to be growing comfortable with me. We rode to church today and spent time together yesterday."

"Good," said McKenzie. "That's important." A look of sadness passed over her face. "Little girls need their fathers."

"I know," Ben whispered. "I'm trying. There are still things I need to figure out."

"I know what it's like not to have a relationship with your father, Ben. It's…important." McKenzie did not meet his eye, and he wanted to reach out and squeeze her arm to comfort her.

"Yes, I know. That's one of the reasons why I'm here."

"Right. I guess I'll see you Tuesday night, then?"

Ben smiled at her. "Tuesday night, yes. Book club? Not so sure."

McKenzie grinned with renewed mischief dancing in her eyes, and he hoped she'd forgotten the questions about whether or not he would stay in town for his little girl.

Chapter Seven

On Tuesday, rain sliced through Kudzu Creek in narrow sheets that fell so fast the back alley behind the diner was a swimming pool by the time McKenzie elbowed the car door open. Thunder growled overhead as she hurried inside, wiping water off her head and shaking her hands and feet. She dried her shoes on a mat and found Barney staring forlornly at a wall covered with sticky notes while he tied a bright white apron across his generous belly. "Is that new?" asked McKenzie in surprise. She hadn't seen it the day before.

He glanced at her sideways. "My old apron had too much personality."

"You've had the same apron for twenty years. That's a part of your charm."

"It's always brought me good luck," the older man lamented.

McKenzie offered Barney a pained smile. "I assume it's another one of Mayer's improvements?"

He nodded miserably. "He gave me this new one last night."

McKenzie patted his shoulder in a comforting gesture. She'd often thought how much happier her life would have been if she'd had a loving and hardworking father like Barney. He toiled behind the scenes with little appreciation and was devoted to his wife and two grown sons as well as several grandchildren. He loved the diner as much as she did. "Everyone appreciates you, Barney," she assured him. "Whether you wear an old, stained apron with character or a crisp, new white one."

He plucked at it with a finger. "It's as stiff as meringue."

McKenzie laughed. "Flipping a few burgers and a good fish fry will break it in."

Barney guffawed and then motioned toward the bulletin board calendar, where several reminders hung. "I'm not going to be at the grill as much as I have been." One notice said *Check Phone App Daily*, which meant the shifts could change at any time. Another read *Welcome, Terry!*

McKenzie squinted and moved closer. "Who's Terry?"

"He's the new hire."

"I thought we weren't getting anyone new."

"Not for wait staff. He's the new cook."

McKenzie reared back. "A new cook? But you're the cook here."

Barney gave her a sad smile. "Apparently, I'm not worth the overtime."

McKenzie exhaled, feeling his frustration. Barney made a noise in his throat and then grumbled, "Change is a good thing. Right?"

She pursed her lips. "Sometimes…maybe, most of the time," she admitted. "But I don't like it." She looked around the kitchen, which was shimmering with new stainless steel cookware. It was uncured, unflavored and charmless. "And I don't do well with it."

"Welp," grunted Barney, snapping a hairnet over his nearly hairless scalp, "at least you can't improve bacon."

McKenzie laughed and grabbed her apron off its hook. Mayer was in the new office that had taken over the break room, but she ignored him and went into the dining room to start the coffee. She found the bitter new brand of java and checked the display case to make sure it was clean before she brought the day-old tarts out. On her way back into the kitchen, Mayer met her at the door with a grim face.

"Did you check your app this morning, Miss Price?"

"No." McKenzie gave him a quizzical look. "I saw the reminder on the bulletin board, but I haven't looked at it since yesterday." She reached for her pocket and realized she didn't have her phone. "My phone's in my handbag."

Mayer sighed as if she was a hopeless case. "If you would have checked your shift app this morning, you would have seen you don't need to come in for another hour."

"But who'd start the coffee?" she pointed out before she could stop herself.

"I'm here, and I can do it." Mayer motioned toward the new espresso machine. "That takes no time at all."

"Most people just want a hot java," McKenzie reminded him, but it fell on deaf ears.

"Tomorrow, make sure to check your app."

"Are the shifts going to change that often?"

Mayer slanted his head at her. "Things move fast in this industry. You'll have to keep up."

McKenzie almost burst into laughter, but she gave Mayer a solemn nod and eased past him as if he had cooties. She stopped at the board and eyeballed the newly posted schedule more closely. Her mouth soured. She had fewer hours than she'd had the week before. It was as if he was whittling away her shifts a little at a time. Fewer hours meant less pay, and less pay meant less savings to invest in the diner when it went up for sale. She and Jill had decided that the Hills putting off the sale of Southern Fried Kudzu wasn't a bad thing; this way, she had more time to save on the down payment.

McKenzie checked Barney's name and saw his hours had diminished as well. He was almost part-time, besides some training time for whoever Terry was. She bristled and made a mental note to call Mr. Hill. She didn't want to be a rat, but after running the diner for so long, she felt she should make sure the owner knew about the changes taking place at his restaurant. After grabbing the tarts and sliding them into the case, McKenzie flipped the Welcome sign over just in time for Diane to dash inside between the raindrops.

"Good morning, everyone," she called. "It's going to be quite a day!"

Barney called out hello from behind the pass-through window. McKenzie padded back to the register. Yes, it was. She counted the hours she had left until she could drive home and change for Claire Ainsworth's dinner party. Her evening meal last night had been a quick can of soup with Bailey, but tonight, they would be treated to a proper dinner at the Ainsworths' historic home, which was known as Henny House. She was looking forward to the evening, and the thought that Megan would be there for Bailey made it even better.

"Do you want tarts this morning?" McKenzie asked with determined cheer while Diane puzzled over the new coffee board.

Her friend pouted and shook her head. "No thanks, McKenzie. They were a little chewy to me yesterday." She snuck a glance through the porthole on the kitchen door. "I'm not sure what a *ristretto* is, so please just pour a black coffee for me.

"As you wish." McKenzie smiled. She'd make sure to report this customer's comments to the new manager.

Claire and Bradley Ainsworth lived on Maple Grove Lane in a beautifully restored Victorian. Ben helped Megan out of the car and then swept his gaze down the charming street, admiring the leafless trees standing guard over flower beds full of late-blooming camellias and mums. They made bright spots of color in the gloom of the oncoming evening. When he climbed the stairs to the yellow veranda and rang the doorbell, the porchlight clicked on, and the door swung open. A familiar little girl with blonde locks looked up at him. "Hello," she said politely; then her face brightened. "Hi, Megan. Do you want to see my room?"

His daughter looked down the hall over her shoulder then shyly down at her feet. "Hi," said Ben warmly. "Do you know Megan from school?"

"Yes, and dance class," said Emily. "She's Bailey's friend, but I'm in kindergarten."

The girls examined each other. "Megan, would you like to play with Emily?" Ben prodded.

"Yes," Emily pleaded, "come play!"

Megan glanced up at Ben, and there was something in her eyes that made his heart melt. "It'll be okay. I'm coming in, too." After a pause, she took Emily's outstretched hand, and before Ben could say goodbye, the girls darted off. Claire appeared then, wiping her hands on a dish towel.

"Oh, good—you made it. Please come inside."

Ben let himself in and realized he understood Megan's nerves completely. He wasn't used to being invited into other people's homes beyond his own family. Occasionally, coworkers would get together, or there'd be parties for the hospital staff, but even then, he stayed on the fringes of the crowd, counting the minutes until he could politely leave. Oblivious to his apprehension, Claire motioned toward the living room, where a newscaster announced the news from a television over a mantel. "Help yourself."

Ben thanked her as Bradley jumped up from the couch, where he'd been conversing with Diane Morris and another mature woman with bobbed, chin-length hair. "Hi, Ben. Come on in."

Ben shook hands with Bradley and took a seat near the window. "This is my aunt, Vi Ainsworth," said Bradley, and Ben jumped to his feet again, feeling foolish. There would be no sitting in corners at Henny House.

"Hello," he said to the elder Mrs. Ainsworth. "I'm Dr. Cooper."

"Yes, *Dr.* Cooper," Bradley corrected himself. "I'm sorry."

Ben realized he sounded pretentious. "Ben is fine, actually."

"He's been Ben for as long as *I* can remember," came a salty tone. Ms. Olivia waggled her fingers in a salute from the other end of the couch. She was wearing a white-and-green sheet of a dress that looked like it'd suit a much larger woman.

"Hello, Ms. Olivia." Ben grinned. Her teasing eased his nerves.

She patted the top of her hairpiece. "Do you see I'm getting around just fine now?"

"That, you are."

Bradley finished the introductions, which included Diane and her husband; his cousin and Ben's old classmate, Donovan Ainsworth; and Donovan's mother and his wife, Lindsey. Then Bradley's uncle, yet another Ainsworth, wandered in with a sports magazine in his grip. Shouts from the back bedrooms pierced the walls. Lindsey bounced a baby boy on her lap and said over the noise, "Our two other boys are in the back with the girls." She had long dark hair and seemed to complement Donovan, who'd sold a law office to become a district attorney.

"Three boys?" he asked, somewhat impressed.

"Yes, well, the two in the back are twins," she admitted.

"The Ainsworth twins from Miss Sherry's dance class," surmised Ben.

Lindsey narrowed her eyes. "How're they doing? Claire takes them."

"They keep it lively," Ben allowed, and Donovan laughed. He asked Ben how his parents were, and they reminisced over an English teacher they'd shared in school. No one said anything about Ben's lack of popularity. The jokes. The name-calling. As talk turned to home renovations on a project Bradley was doing one street over, Ben caught himself looking out the window for McKenzie. He almost stood when he saw the headlights of a compact car race up to the curb. McKenzie and Bailey hopped out and hurried up the walkway, chatting. McKenzie looked serious, her hair swinging around her shoulders and her gaze lowered to the ground. Concern pricked the back of Ben's neck when the doorbell rang. "I can get that," he offered. Bradley nodded, and Ben stepped into the foyer and opened the door. "Hello."

"Hi, Dr. Cooper," said Bailey. "This isn't your house."

He laughed. "No, it's not. How did you guess?"

"Because Emily lives here, duh."

"Bailey!" McKenzie widened her eyes. "Be respectful, please."

"I'm sorry, Dr. Cooper," apologized Bailey without a hitch. She glanced past him as if anxious to leave the adults behind.

"Come in," he welcomed her. "Megan is in the back room with Emily."

"Yes!" cheered Bailey, and she skipped away.

McKenzie stepped inside. "Thank you. I'm sorry about that."

"It's no problem," Ben assured her. "She's just six, after all."

"Plus twenty," chuckled McKenzie. "She actually turns seven in a few weeks, and don't you forget it."

Ben laughed and motioned toward the living room, but touched her elbow as she started in. "Are you okay?"

"Sure. Why?"

"There's just something... You seem tired," he finished.

McKenzie gave him a curious look, but Ben noticed her quiet exhale as they walked into the living room. "It was just a weird day at the diner."

"I'm sorry." He offered his seat and sat on a plush rug on the floor, and everyone quizzed McKenzie on the new espresso machine at Southern Fried Kudzu until Claire ordered them all into the kitchen for dinner. They filled their plates buffet-style while chatting and joking. Then the senior Mr. and Mrs. Ainsworth and Diane went out to eat on the well-lit front porch, which had a gazebo attached to one end. The kids begged to eat in the back at a picnic table Bradley had built out of an old pallet. When McKenzie decided to sit on the back porch with the kids, Ben returned to the living room so she didn't think he'd come only to see her. Ms. Olivia padded over beside him to where he'd moved onto the couch. He quickly rose. "Please, take my seat," he offered.

"Thank you, Doctor," she teased. "Just what an old woman needs."

"Let me find another chair," Claire insisted.

Ben held up a hand. "No, it's okay. I think I'll watch Megan and her friends." He found his way out a back door through the kitchen hoping McKenzie didn't think he was following her. The front porch wrapped around to the backyard, which was dotted with lawn chairs and even a hammock. Ben sat near the steps, where he could keep an eye on the children running around in the grass in the remains of the evening light. McKenzie was a few feet away, sitting at a table, wrapped in a sweater and munching on a carrot stick, lost in thought. She caught him studying her, and he quickly turned to look at the food on his plate in the glow of a flickering lantern. "There're so many of them," he joked as she walked over and pulled up a chair beside him. "I feel like I'm behind schedule."

"You? I thought I'd have a pair before I

turned thirty. But here I am…" She trailed off. "It's taking longer than I thought," she admitted, "to get where I thought I was supposed to be."

"There's nothing wrong with that," Ben assured her. "I'm just now ready to dive into my career." He turned back to his plate as she fell silent.

After taking a sip from a red plastic cup, she said, "Yes. Claire and Bradley have Emily. The twins and baby are Lindsey and Donovan's, and Jill has Bailey, although my niece and Megan seem to come as a set these days."

Ben remembered Megan's anxious query about the sleepover with her friend the night before when he'd tucked her into bed. "She asked me about the sleepover Friday."

"Bailey won't let us forget about it," admitted McKenzie. "Do you think Megan would be comfortable staying with us overnight?"

"I think so. Her grandma explained what a sleepover was, and she seemed excited. We told her she could call home anytime, and one of us would come get her."

"Let's let them try, then," suggested McKenzie.

Ben didn't fight back a smile. "I think she'll do okay. She doesn't mind me taking her to school anymore or to dance, and we talk a little. Her class is reading *Chicken Little*. Last night, she read me a page."

"That's great progress." McKenzie took a bite out of the baked macaroni Claire had promised she'd make. "Um, this is delicious."

"It's amazing."

"Not quite what you get in Chicago, is it?"

He grinned. "I'm sure it's there, but the South has a cuisine all its own."

"Don't you miss it at all?" pressed McKenzie.

"A little bit," Ben admitted. "My instruments, my stereo system, CDs, the old albums…"

"You still have your albums?" McKenzie set her fork on her plate and dabbed her lips with a napkin. "Sometimes I get nostalgic for The Rembrandts, but they just don't sound the same streaming from a website."

"I know what you mean," Ben agreed. "Some things are better left a few steps behind technology."

McKenzie jerked her head in agreement. "That's why I'm so grumpy tonight. Things are changing a little too fast at the diner."

"How so?"

"Mr. Hill's nephew has an online scheduling program, new bakeware and he's even taken fried kudzu off the menu."

"No!" Ben teased.

McKenzie rolled her eyes. "I'm serious. Barney and I came up with fried kudzu after they updated the menu years ago. Lots of people order the fried kudzu, chickpeas and rice every day. Not everyone wants a burger."

"Don't you make the tarts? Darlene said you did."

"I did until this month. Now it's whoever's on shift Monday mornings, whether they've ever done it before or not. He's changed everything." McKenzie frowned.

"To be fair, it's a business," Ben pointed out. "Is it working?"

"I don't know. I don't count the till anymore, and he keeps the credit card receipts. I can't say we're less busy, but I've had my share of complaints." McKenzie exhaled heavily. "Mayer doesn't have to deal with them because he's in his office most of the time."

"I'm sorry." Ben noticed her eyes looked wet at the corners. He wished he could wrap an arm around her for comfort, but she might take it the wrong way. "Maybe you could find another diner somewhere else," he suggested.

McKenzie pushed her plate back. "I don't want to go anywhere else. You know Kudzu Creek is home to me."

A sudden shout rose in the air. Ben looked out into the yard and grinned. The Ainsworth twins were chasing the girls. He turned back to McKenzie, who still looked somber. "What about Atlanta?" he pressed. "There're all kinds of eclectic and unique options there. I bet they'd pay more, too."

McKenzie shook her head. "No. I know working in a diner wasn't my life's ambition, but after I started there, everything just seemed to fall into place. I've been there so long and know everyone so well—it feels like the perfect fit. Or it did. Mayer has ruined everything, and my hours have been cut, too."

"I don't know what else to tell you except to wait him out. Eventually, Mr. Hill is going to sell, right?"

"That's the plan." McKenzie sighed. "But until then, I don't know what to do. Lose myself in books, I guess, when I'm not doing laundry." She sat back, and he resisted the urge to grab her hand and squeeze it. Once upon a time, they could talk about anything, and she seemed to need that from him, he thought—perhaps now more than ever.

"Well, maybe now's the time," Ben said carefully.

"For what?"

"To do something bigger, like you always wanted to."

"You mean a bookstore."

"If you still want one."

McKenzie stared into the darkening sky. "All I ever wanted was a normal family and a little shop, but they were both just fantasies. I have Jill and Bailey, but where would I find space in Kudzu Creek for a store? There's nothing available."

"Fantasies are just dreams we convince ourselves are impossible," he assured her. "Make it your Christmas wish, and imagine what can happen if you believe."

McKenzie snorted. "You never thought becoming a doctor was a fantasy. I admire that."

"You do?"

"Yes. Even though you left town," she admitted. "I still think you should come home now if you're done with your schooling. Your parents and child are here."

Silence settled over them, and Ben leaned forward to watch the kids play. The temperature had dropped several degrees, and he shivered. At least, that's what he told himself was the reason for the chill. McKenzie didn't understand him. There was still more to conquer. He could go higher, accomplish more, and this was the perfect time in his life to do it. It'd never happen in a small town like Kudzu Creek—a place where he would always walk in his father's footsteps and be haunted by the ghosts of his past—ghosts who looked a lot like Scotty and Billy. Megan would be fine. She was doing better than he had been at her age. "No," he muttered gruffly. "The backcountry life is not for me."

"Country? I think you mean *simple*. And that car, by the way…" McKenzie began.

Ben opened his mouth to resume the same old argument they'd had since they were old enough to apply to colleges. "Daddy!" A familiar voice pulled his attention back to the yard. Megan stood a few feet away, staring directly at him with a look of excited expectation.

Daddy.

"Daddy, watch!" She turned sideways, raised her arms over her head and did a wobbly cartwheel in the moonlight.

"You did it!" shrieked Bailey, who began to hop up and down beside her. She threw her arms around her friend as if she'd just completed a marathon.

"That was great, Megan!" McKenzie called out. "I'm so proud of you!"

Ben jumped to his feet and stumbled into the

withered grass that hinted summer had come and gone. Fall had left its mark. The seasons were changing, which meant life was turning its pages, too. He turned on the flashlight on his phone and put his daughter in the spotlight. "Do it again, Megan. That was amazing!"

Chapter Eight

Friday, at Miss Sherry's Dance Studio, McKenzie and Ben whispered back and forth about their quiet Thanksgivings and the leftovers they were facing while the children practiced for their upcoming holiday recital. Ben admitted he was enjoying his few days off, which prompted McKenzie to tell him about the unhappy lines of customers at Southern Fried Kudzu. Even though the diner had new staff, it was ill-equipped to handle the new changes, especially while Barney was trying to train the new cook from Ryan's House, a county rehabilitation program. McKenzie liked Terry, she assured Ben, and believed everyone deserved a chance, but the constant backup was driving her insane. More and more tarts sat longer in the pastry case, and recent reviews on social media were not all positive anymore.

After dance class was over, they waved goodbye to Claire and the other parents and then walked outside to the parking lot together. McKenzie helped Bailey buckle in while Ben grabbed Megan's overnight duffel bag and blanket from his car. The little girl shuffled her feet in the gravel until McKenzie invited her to climb into her back seat. After assuring Ben that Megan would be watched over, she drove the girls home, hoping Jill had come up with something fun for dinner. Her sister pulled through. With lots of giggles and excitement, they ate hot dogs and corn chips and then watched a girl-detective movie. Afterward, McKenzie provided everyone with flashlights so they could make animal shadows and do skits. When Bailey finally began to wind down and a blissful Megan looked drowsy, McKenzie and Jill carried them to the double bed in McKenzie's room. Rather than take Bailey's single, McKenzie told her sister good-night and laid out on the couch.

Crickets slurred out a warning that winter would soon be upon them with biting, snowless days full of leaden skies and the occasional blustery rain shower. But for now, the house felt peaceful as it snuggled her little family and Bailey's friend. McKenzie let herself relax. Despite all the turmoil at work, she looked forward to Christmas and the moments she'd share with her family and friends. She needed to choose joy. To find it again. It would be special for Megan, too, with her father back in town. She reminded McKenzie so much of Ben. Although she seemed to have her mother's eyes, her dusty brown locks hinted that Chetana was not a redhead. Megan was a quiet, thoughtful girl—and very quick—but unlike Ben, she was less guarded toward gestures of friendship or activities. She was not a social butterfly by any means, but she certainly enjoyed the company of others, fearing new experiences more than any criticism.

McKenzie smiled to herself. If Ben had taken dance, he would have practiced until his toes bled and made a pact with himself to perform on Broadway. She'd always admired his quiet courage and fearless ambition. Despite being bullied while growing up, he had never let anything diminish his belief in what he could do. The only problem was, he held his father on a pedestal of perfection and seemed to expect nothing less for himself—as if good behavior could shield him from life's bumps and bruises. McKenzie rolled over to face the couch cushion. She'd been raised in a family quite different from his, although she always believed she would have her own someday. So why hadn't it happened? Because she was afraid, she admitted with a heavy exhale. Not of criticism, like Ben, but afraid that growing up without a healthy relationship with her parents meant she could never be a good one herself. Maybe she was afraid to pursue a serious relationship because that would mean taking a chance on someone who might be less than loving, kind or encouraging.

Megan was fortunate to have her grandparents in her life, McKenzie thought wistfully. Maybe things weren't ideal, but McKenzie knew Ben. He would be there for Megan. She was special, like her dad. McKenzie stared unseeing into the dark. Her thoughts drifted to Ben… He was gentle and kind, and he treated others with respect. His patience was as unyielding as his quiet determination. And, she admitted, heart tingling against her will, he was a handsome man. It was too bad he didn't feel like he belonged in Kudzu Creek, because he'd once thought he belonged with her.

"Grandma!" The cry in the dark made McKenzie bolt upright.

"Megan!" She scrambled off the couch and came down with a crash on her knees but jumped back up and rushed to her bedroom. In the dim light of the stars outside the window, she could make out the outline of a child sitting up. "Megan?" McKenzie whispered. There was a sob. McKenzie stepped lightly over to the mattress and sank down beside her. "What's wrong, honey? It's me, McKenzie. I'm here." There was a strained silence until McKenzie offered her open arms, and the little girl climbed into her lap, sniffling quietly. "Did you wake up and feel confused?"

The shadow nodded. She patted the little girl's back. "It's okay, baby. You're safe. Bailey is right beside you, and I'm here." The child shuddered and clutched her tightly. "We love you, Megan, and you don't have to be afraid. Okay?"

Nothing.

"Do you want me to call your mom?" Before McKenzie could correct herself and say *grandmother*, the little girl whispered, "I don't have a mom. She lives far away."

"Your daddy's here."

Another sniffle. "He's not a real daddy."

"Yes, he is," McKenzie assured her with a sinking heart. "He just lives far away."

"Poppy is here."

"Yes, Poppy is your grandpa, but Ben is your

father. He'll come get you, if you want me to call him."

"I want my grandma," whimpered Megan. "She makes me hot chocolate when I wake up in the dark."

"Okay, let's give her a call. I'll explain what happened to Bailey in the morning."

"No!" the child blurted . She clutched McKenzie tightly. "Bailey will be sad when she wakes up if I'm gone. Can you stay with us in this room?"

"Sure, I can. And your daddy will be here in the morning."

"At breakfast?"

"Yes. He promised, remember?"

Megan nodded to herself. Ben had promised he would see her bright and early when he'd told her goodbye. The little girl just needed more reassurance.

"If I know anything, Ben Cooper is a man of his word, sweetheart. If he said he'll be here, he'll be here. He's one of the best men I know."

Megan seemed comforted and, after a few long minutes, nodded off beside her. McKenzie stretched out on the foot of the bed, heart heavy. Megan obviously didn't think she had any parents, not real ones. It was a complicated situation, and maybe that's why she was so unsure at times. McKenzie closed her eyes sadly, wondering how many years it would be before Ben came home or if he would at all. Her eyes dampened when she thought of the time and space between her and her own parents. What would Megan do when the man she was beginning to accept left again, even if it was to care for other people? It would break her heart, realized McKenzie, and her eyes flooded with tears for the little girl who would have to say goodbye to her father once more. She let them stream down her face as a quiet voice in the back of her head suggested she might be crying a little for herself. She didn't just want him to stay for Megan—she wanted him in her life, too.

After he picked Megan up on Saturday morning, and thanked McKenzie profusely, Ben spent the next few hours, helping his little girl feed the chickens, dogs and Jiminy. They laughed over the donkey's excited brays as Ben questioned her about her first sleepover. She assured him it'd been fun as she steepled her hands together and showed him how McKenzie had taught her to make a shadow that looked like a duck.

"I hope that doesn't give you any ideas," he

chuckled, "because I think you have enough animals."

"I know." Megan smiled. "And they're a lot of work. Sometimes…" She lowered her voice, as if ashamed her grandparents might overhear. "I'd really like a kitten to sleep with me in my bed."

"Kittens take work, too," Ben explained.

"Like what?" Dangling a carrot for Jiminy, Megan looked up innocently.

"They have to be fed every day, brushed and—" Ben held up a finger "—you have to clean out a litter box because they don't go outside."

"That's not so bad," Megan said, and Ben realized that after farm animals, cleaning up for a cat was nothing. "I have a neighbor," he began, "in the apartment across the hall that has a giant Dalmatian." He spanned his hands, and her eyes widened with interest. His phone chose to interrupt them at that moment, and Megan shoved the carrot into Jiminy's mouth and watched him crunch. "I'll be right back," whispered Ben. He stepped a distance away toward the chicken coop. "Dr. Cooper."

"Ben, this is Darlene. Sorry I didn't call your daddy, but you said to phone you if there were any emergencies."

"Is everything okay?"

"It's old Mr. Dougherty. His wife called all in a flap because he's dizzy and won't get out of bed. She wants to drive him to the emergency room in Albany, but he refuses to leave the house. Says he just needs to rest."

Ben's mind raced as he tried to recall Dougherty's last visit. "If I remember right, his blood pressure is high."

"Yes, I'm looking at his chart," said Darlene. "We were just down the road at the market, so I popped into the clinic and pulled it for you."

"Thanks for fielding my calls on your weekend." Ben frowned. "This could be a warning sign of something worse. I think he better come in. I can be at the clinic in a few minutes." He glanced across the yard at Megan.

"I don't think he'll come, but I'll call his wife. You may want to wait."

Ben made a noise under his breath. His father wasn't above making a house call now and then, and although this was a new century, it seemed like the best thing to do if the crusty patient was going to be stubborn. His stern-doctor tone kicked in. "Tell Mrs. Dougherty I will be at their door as soon as I can get there. Can you text me their address?"

"Sure thing, Dr. Cooper," said Darlene with

obvious relief. "I know she'll calm down if someone will go out and talk to the old fool. Even his son can't get him to move."

Ben ended the call, his mind focused on emergency treatments for high blood pressure. Stubborn men like Mr. Dougherty often lived shorter lives. With a frown, he hurried over to Megan, who was whispering over the fence to her donkey. "I have to go help someone who's hurting, Megan. I'll be back later, okay?"

"Okay, Daddy." She looked up at him with soft-hazel eyes. "That's what you do, isn't it? Help people so they don't hurt?"

A sudden lump tightened in Ben's throat. "Yes, honey. I help sick people get better."

She looked at Jiminy. "Jiminy was sick once, and Poppy called a doctor to come out and help him."

"Yes, there are different kinds of doctors for animals. Grandpa and I don't do that kind of medicine."

"Oh." She looked at her donkey's big eyes and crooned, "Poor Jiminy. He swallowed a part of a nail, but he's better."

Ben saw just how big her heart was, and it filled him with pride. "Maybe you can be an animal doctor someday."

Megan shook her head as the animal nuzzled

her hand, and she murmured something under her breath.

"What's that?"

She looked up with innocent eyes. "I want to be a dancer."

He grinned at her. "Then you will be the best dancer in the entire world."

She beamed. "The best in Kudzu Creek—and I'll make people happy."

Ben realized with a start that to Megan, Kudzu Creek was the entire world. She had no idea that there were opportunities he could provide for her in a bigger city if she lived with him. "Okay, then. We'll talk about it when I get back. Someone is really sick, so I need to go."

Less than thirty minutes later he arrived at an old house southeast of his parents' place that looked vaguely familiar. Ben turned into a packed-clay driveway crowded with vehicles that looked like they hadn't been driven in some time. He climbed out of the car, embarrassed he'd driven the sports car instead of his father's pickup truck, and smoothed down his jeans, relieved he hadn't changed. A collared shirt and jeans were presentable enough for a house call. He reached for the backpack he'd thrown in with a few supplies, his pulse racing. It was the excitement of the chance to figure out what made someone tick, or what kept them from tickingproperly, that fulfilled him. A medical mystery was a puzzle to be solved, and he got to help people along the way.

He studied the small ranch house with peeling gray paint. Faded flowers had wilted into dark lumps in an overgrown flower bed. A footpath led to a sagging screen door. It swung open, and Scotty Dougherty lumbered out, shouting something over his shoulder, his face in its perpetual scowl. Ben froze mid-step. Dougherty. *Of course*. He hadn't made the connection. The grumpy Mr. Dougherty at the clinic was Scotty Dougherty's father.

So many patients filed through his life with names that didn't stick in his mind the way symptoms and solutions did, but this time, it mattered. Scotty was halfway to him before he noticed the sports car, then swiveled to see Ben a few feet away.

"You're the doctor."

"My father's laid up," Ben said stiffly.

"Oh." A range of emotions morphed across Scotty's face. "Well, good luck," he said in a caustic tone. "You're gonna need it." He stomped by, and Ben didn't look back, grateful he was leaving. With a sharp inhale that stabbed his diaphragm, Ben continued on to the tired screen door and knocked. A woman with short, brassy hair and a thick layer of makeup on her creased face opened it.

"Oh," she said with relief, "I thought you were the neighbor." The growl of a pickup truck backing out of the driveway interrupted her. She stood up on her toes. "Scotty's leaving already, huh?" She clucked her tongue and looked back at Ben with a weary expression. "His father wouldn't let him call the ambulance. You must be Dr. Cooper's son."

"Yes, I'm Bentley Cooper," Ben replied, and in the back of his mind, he wondered if she'd heard his name spoken in ridicule in the past. She didn't hesitate, but opened the door and said, "Please come in."

He brushed past her into a small family room with an outdated couch and a comfortable-looking recliner parked in front of a television. The room was clean and orderly, and there were statues of geese poised on wooden shelves that reminded him of his loving grandmother. "How is your husband, Mrs. Dougherty?"

She hurried ahead to lead him down a hall. "He's so dizzy he can't get up, and he won't eat or drink anything." Ben went down the list of questions he knew he should ask, and she answered promptly, her voice tight with concern.

When she pushed open a door into a bedroom, he saw a sizeable lump under a blanket move on the bed. "Honey, it's Dr. Cooper."

Mr. Dougherty grunted and pulled the blanket down so he could see. He scowled at his first sight of Ben. "That ain't the doc, Becky, that's his boy."

"I am a doctor, Mr. Dougherty," said Ben firmly. He'd treated old curmudgeons in the emergency room lots of times and learned from watching the more experienced nurses how to handle them. "I know I'm not what you're used to, but I'm as qualified as my father." It was hard not to notice the pictures of children on the walls around the room that included a young Scotty, wearing a baseball uniform, football uniform or smirking in his graduation cap and gown. Ben's stomach lurched, and he took a deep breath. "In fact," he continued, "I just finished my surgical residence."

Mr. Dougherty squeezed his eyes shut as if the conversation was too much. "I don't need no surgery," he grumbled.

"I'd like to check you out," insisted Ben. "For my dad, and to see what you do need. I've worked with stroke patients before, and you're showing some of the signs."

Mrs. Dougherty sucked in a breath beside him. "Please, Harold," she whispered.

He grunted. "Fine, but I'm not getting up. The world is spinning."

"You don't have to," Ben assured him. He held back a sigh of relief and gave Mrs. Dougherty a triumphant smile.

"Thank you so much," she whispered in a low tone. "I don't know what I'd have done if you hadn't come." Her relief was mingled with sincere gratitude, and when their eyes met, she smiled back.

Ben thought of his talk with Megan and murmured, "You're welcome," touched by her kind words. It wasn't dancing, but he went to work.

Chapter Nine

With only a four-hour shift scheduled on Monday, McKenzie realized she'd have plenty of time to go to book club, so she hurried home after the lunch rush and grabbed her book. Pulling up to the Azalea Inn situated a block from the town's main street, she counted three cars and hoped Claire would make it, because they hadn't had time to talk since the wonderful preholiday dinner party. McKenzie smiled, wondering if Ben would come, too, but she suspected he'd probably forgotten about it. They'd only exchanged a few words at church the day before, and neither had mentioned it Saturday when he'd picked up his daughter after her sleepover.

McKenzie sat in the car, admiring the Christmas decorations that had sprouted overnight up and down Pebble Stretch Road. She didn't see Ben's car and McKenzie herself for looking for it. They'd had plenty of time to talk last Saturday. He'd picked up Megan, remarking how he'd forgotten what a beautiful drive it was out to the house, and admired Tim's medals on the wall—all without commenting on her old pajamas and mismatched socks. He'd been dressed in a pair of running shorts and a sweatshirt, but she averted her attention to his daughter as she gave him a sheepish, welcoming smile while gathering Megan's blanket and backpack. As the girls had said their goodbyes, McKenzie led him to the kitchen and explained about the near-crisis and how she'd gotten Megan back to sleep, but she left out some of the details. They'd parted ways considering the event a success despite the nightmare, but in the back of her mind, McKenzie knew she should have told Ben about the conversation she'd had with Megan about not having real parents. What point was there, though, when he was so bent on returning to Chicago? Megan would have to get used to living estranged from her parents for now. At least, McKenzie thought with determination, she could empathize and be there for her. Just talking to Ben about his leaving made her uptight, and she didn't want to strain their new friendship. McKenzie noticed movement in the inn's windows, scooped up her book, and hurried inside to her friends and the book club buffet.

"Look at this gingerbread-jam croissant!" cried Diane.

Vi Ainsworth ripped into one with a big bite. "These are spicy and delicious," she moaned.

McKenzie could hardly wait to dive in. "I always look forward to your baking, Lindsey— more than I do the book, to be honest."

"I loved your choice for this month," Lindsey assured her. "There's just something fascinating about Napoleon. He was a complicated man."

"Aren't they all?" declared Diane, and everyone smiled.

"No more than us, I suppose," chimed in Claire.

McKenzie suddenly remembered the questions she had about young children and sleep terrors, but the door to the lobby swung open, and the *rat-tat-tat* of a cane announced Ms. Olivia's arrival. "Look who I've brought with me," she announced.

Everyone's faces split into grins, and Claire laughed. McKenzie looked over her shoulder, and her stomach did a somersault. Ben stood beside Ms. Olivia with a sheepish grin on his face. He met McKenzie's eyes and gave a little shrug, although the flush on his cheeks made her curious. "I'm on a lunch break."

"You mean *brunch* break." Diane waved a croissant. "This is Second Breakfast."

"That's not fair," complained Lindsey, looking sideways at her mother-in-law. "I can't get Donovan to give up his lunch hour."

"Bradley won't even open a book!" laughed Claire. "He prefers the movie version."

"Not everyone likes to read novels," said Vi. "Come in, Dr. Cooper. We want to hear your great literary thoughts."

"I'm not sure I have any," Ben confessed. He escorted Ms. Olivia through the inn's dining room, which was strung with silver garland and little blue bulbs across its dark peach walls.

"You have a cane," McKenzie observed as Mrs. Olivia approached the table.

"That, I do," she said, wagging it in the air. "That's why Dr. Cooper is here. He gave me this thing this morning and wants to follow me around town to make sure I don't hurt anybody."

"Or yourself," said Ben, pulling out the chair next to McKenzie for her.

Mrs. Olivia glanced at it, looked at McKenzie and then took a step toward the remaining chair next to Diane. She looked up innocently at

Ben. "I need to sit closer to the pastries. You'll have to sit here, by this pretty girl."

McKenzie looked down at the book in her hands, hoping her cheeks hadn't reddened. There was a slight pause over the table; then Claire said, "Okay, so who found this fictional account of Napoleon believable?"

Voices lifted in protest while Ben took his seat beside McKenzie. She caught a faint whiff of something earthy and woodsy. A perfect winter cologne, subtle but alluring. She handed him a dessert plate, and he thanked her, filling it and listening quietly to the conversation about the pride of man and only speaking when asked his opinion. When Ms. Olivia quoted Hugh Blair's "Pride makes us esteem ourselves; vanity makes us desire the esteem of others," he froze so noticeably that McKenzie waited for him to speak. His eyes were on the table, but his thoughts were far away, and she wanted to reach out and bring him back. Ben had drifted off to some corner of his mind that he'd retreated to. McKenzie let out a quiet sigh, yearning to be alone with him to hear his honest opinion that she suspected he was keeping to himself for some reason. She wanted to spend more time with him outside of the book club, she realized— more time than at the dance studio, the diner or even at Claire's house. But of course, that would mean… She forced herself to focus on the conversation about the book at hand. Ben was a doctor and a father, and a very good friend—to everyone. He'd never been more than that to her, and with his plans to leave again, more would never happen. For the first time in her life, this made McKenzie feel incredibly disappointed.

She found herself following him out the door as everyone waved goodbye and drifted into the tepid, sunny day. Claire had offered to drive Ms. Olivia home since she lived across the street from Henny House, and Diane had to hurry off to reopen her shop. She'd asked about Mayer, and McKenzie confided that her hours had been cut.

"Well, that'll save your feet," Claire had pointed out, but McKenzie had only nodded in semi-agreement.

Out in the sunshine, she caught up with Ben and walked silently beside him. He motioned toward his sports car. "I'd offer you a ride home, but you have yours here."

"You have to get back to the clinic." She waved him off. "Besides, I'm already done at the diner. I just went home because we're in the middle of washing bedding this week, and I wanted to start the Crock-Pot for Jill."

"That was nice of you."

"She works just as hard as I do." McKenzie dug through her handbag for her keys. "Actually, more these days. It's harder now because I have less hours, so she takes every opportunity she can get for overtime."

Ben looked at her with concern. "Is that going to be a problem?"

"No, it's fine. We don't have a mortgage because it was paid off with Tim's death benefits."

"What a tender mercy after such a tragedy."

McKenzie stopped beside her car and glanced at his ride parked right behind her. "Yes, it was. She bought a van, too. I, unfortunately—"she chuckled, patting the roof of her car "—am still driving vintage, as you so kindly observed. Not that I need a van."

"Can't get a soccer team in there, huh?"

"Nope." McKenzie smiled. "Or a dance team. But I can fit two girls in there, unlike someone's sports car."

Ben laughed. "Thanks for offering to pick up Megan tomorrow after school for us, by the way. Mom wants to go to the cardiologist with Dad."

"She explained why, and it isn't a problem." McKenzie enjoyed cranking up the radio and singing pop songs with the girls while she drove Megan home to the Cooper farm after school.

Ben leaned against the hood, and McKenzie caught another whiff of his scent. The copper in his hair shined in the sun, making his eyes glow. With his coolly casual clothes and clean-shaven jawline, he looked like a model in a car commercial, and it made McKenzie's hands feel weird, as if little crackles of electricity were dancing back and forth along the lines of her palms. She wiped them on her jeans.

"She called you before asking me about it, and I feel like I should apologize," Ben admitted.

"Don't," McKenzie reiterated. "I'm going to pick up Bailey, anyway. I hardly know what to do now, with Mayer shortening my workday."

"You have to fight for what you want," Ben reminded her. "Even if the sale of the diner has been put off, don't let the new manager push you around. Demand that he give you more hours—tell him that people are used to seeing you there. You *are* Southern Fried Kudzu," he said with sincerity, and McKenzie's heart danced at his uplifting compliment.

"I could, I guess," she admitted. "It's just, everyone else there is trying to adapt, and I don't want to rock the boat."

"Why not?"

"It's a good job," she sputtered. "I want to be there."

Ben furrowed his brow, thinking. "Maybe fewer hours means you can consider doing something else now."

McKenzie shifted her weight onto one leg. "Please don't mention the bookstore again."

"Why not?" Ben raised his brows. "You just spent over an hour schooling us on a great novel and letting everyone know which new releases will be bestsellers next year. They'll make great gifts for Christmas." He tilted his head. "How do you find so much time to read, anyway?"

McKenzie smiled through her frustration. Ben still believed she should risk everything. "On breaks. After dinner. Before sleep. Sometimes in the morning with breakfast, if I have a few minutes."

"You always were a big bookworm," he teased.

McKenzie chuckled. "Maybe I should see if they have any part-time openings at the library, but I know they prefer volunteers."

"If it'd make you happy. You'd be a pro."

"I can't be happy all the time," McKenzie argued. "I have to make a living and take care of my family."

"You're doing that now," he chided. "Why not dare to do a little more?"

"Nope," she said stubbornly. "It's not safe.

I know what you're hinting at. A bookstore wouldn't make it in this town, Ben. Not with a library. New books are expensive—and like I said, there isn't any real estate around here that would work. The diner is my only and best option."

"Nothing in life is ever a sure thing," Ben reminded her. "When I got my first failing grade in my freshman year of college I thought it was all over."

"But you rebounded," McKenzie reminded him.

Ben stared at the ground. "You know I was scared to leave town, don't you? Scared to be alone. Scared to fail."

"You've never failed at anything you set your mind to," insisted McKenzie.

"Sure I have. I just kept going. But it was hard without…"

McKenzie had a sudden flashback of Ben being pushed around by older kids in second grade. "You've always gotten back up on your feet, Ben."

"But I don't avoid getting knocked down. I take chances." His words stung.

"And I don't?"

He found her eyes and stared deeply into them. It made her warm all over. "No one can accuse you of not playing it safe."

"I guess," McKenzie admitted. "But at least I don't run away when I get hurt to try to prove something."

"What's that supposed to mean?"

"Well, Ben, you did walk away. You left town."

"To get an education."

McKenzie's throat knotted. "To prove everyone wrong. And you never came back."

"Chicago is my home," he said, his tone cool. "I'm needed there."

"Yes, I know." McKenzie couldn't help but think of Megan. A surge of frustration shot through her. "You should know that when your daughter stayed with us last Friday, she told me she didn't have real parents. That her mother lived far away and you're not around, either."

Ben stiffened. "Yes, I live far away, and she knows that. And I do want kids. I want her. It's just…a process. I'm not ready to be a single dad, and my parents do a better job."

"Says who?" McKenzie shot back. When he offered no response, she said, "Certainly not Megan. I've seen her blossom since you've been here. She speaks up more. She smiles. She's dancing!"

"I'm proud of her," Ben admitted. "We've always talked once a week, with a lot of help from Mom—but if she starts having a hard time with things after this, I'll call her every day."

"If you think that's enough." McKenzie wondered why she felt so desperate. "But she needs you, and she's not the only one."

"You mean people like Harold Dougherty? Trust me, they'd easily pick my dad over me," Ben muttered, "Not everyone here needs me."

"Megan does and so do your folks. Ms. Olivia seems to prefer you, for sure. And look how you've helped Bailey. The people that matter do."

He looked up at her, eyes darkening to mahogany. "It's the people that matter I'm trying to figure out."

When Ben returned to the office, he was not only late but slightly fuming and confused. What had started as a charming luncheon had turned into a guilt trip. *Vanity?* Was that why Ms. Olivia had invited him to discuss a book about Napoleon? *I'm nothing like that warmonger,* he thought stubbornly. He'd dedicated his life to serving his fellow man, just like his dad. And yes, he liked the accolades, but that didn't make him a bad person—or a bad father.

Happy holiday music blared over the speakers in the waiting room, and he mumbled a greeting to Mindy before heading to the office and plopping into his chair behind the desk. Then there was McKenzie. Her energy matched his frequency and drew him to her like a magnet. She could have been the puzzle piece that completed him, but for some reason, they just couldn't connect. Besides his parents, she was the only person he trusted to speak honestly to him, and yet she wouldn't take his advice to try something besides the diner. She could be frozen forever in her safe place—afraid to move on or move forward if she refused to let go of what her parents did to her. Life had knocked her down, and she had no intention of getting back up on her feet and running a race where she might take another emotional tumble. Her pleading on behalf of Megan had seared his conscience.

Ben glanced at his watch and jumped up to hurry into the hall. He found a frowning Darlene who handed him a file, and he dashed into the first room. Jill and Bailey Price sat on the examination table together and looked up in surprise. "Oh, you're back," said Jill. "The nurse said you were helping Ms. Olivia with something."

"I'm sorry," Ben apologized, trying to balance his emotions. "The meeting ran long."

"Meeting?"

"Book club."

"You read books?" asked Bailey in surprise.

"All the time," he joked. "Ms. Olivia needed an escort." He grinned at Jill but didn't mention the books he read were medical journals, in which he hoped to see his name in print someday. They discussed Bailey's progress, and he hurried into the hall to order the new prescription she needed before returning with a sticker.

"Thank you," said Jill, putting a hand on his arm. "I love your dad, but we've had some disagreements over how to treat her asthma. The allergy test you ordered explained a lot, and this emergency inhaler seems to be working."

"Sometimes it's a team effort."

"You're right." She studied him. "So how much longer before you leave?"

He shifted his gaze. "Through Christmas, when my dad should be well enough to come into the office."

"Your family must be very appreciative."

"Yes," he acknowledged, "they are."

Jill smiled. "I know this is what you always hoped for. I remember how hard you studied when you were in school."

"It is what I've always wanted," Ben agreed, feeling at last like someone understood him.

"You don't miss it here, though? I know sometimes, what we want changes as time goes by."

"No." Ben hesitated, then said, "I like the city lights. The buzz. The anonymity… I mean, I did when I was a resident."

"You've come a long way." She shook her head, seeming impressed. "I'm glad you're happy."

"Well, I don't love the weather," Ben said. "And I do miss winding roads and fields of something besides corn." He chuckled. "Not that I saw a lot of farms living in the city." He had enjoyed his return to the slow pace of Kudzu Creek, people like the Doughertys notwithstanding.

"I'm sure glad you came when you did." Jill stood up with a grateful smile. "This has changed everything for Bailey, and it could have taken a lot longer. So thank you."

"You're welcome." Her touch filled him with quiet joy. It was like when he came out of surgery and someone threw themselves into his embrace and cried with gratitude. Only this was better. He'd helped someone he knew personally, and that meant more. His throat knotted when he imagined Bailey growing into a healthy, active young woman. He would be a very tiny part of that.

After their goodbyes, something gnawed at Ben while he finished the appointments for the day. He pondered the highway as he started home, considering how it snaked around the tall, browning grass. That morning's frost had hinted at the holidays and family time to come. He'd missed so many of them while he was off pursuing his career. Now he had one, and a chance for a fellowship, but was staying in a big city worth it? Could he find greatness in a small town in Georgia?

The car shuddered as he rounded a curve, and Ben decelerated. It was easy to drive too fast in a vehicle like this. A ray of sunshine shifted in the clouds, blinding him, so he slowed further to see clearly around him. The trees were changing—accepting their destiny and what God wanted for them. Withered leaves danced in the breeze. Soon they would come to a stop and decay, a process that would allow the earth to provide nourishment for new seeds to come. Their saplings would grow into trees.

Megan flashed in Ben's mind, dancing through a life under the Georgia sun, and his eyes watered without warning. She needed a sun—something or someone for her universe to orbit around so she wouldn't drift off into places that might lead her down difficult or dangerous paths. Ben thought of the emergency room rotation he'd worked and the lost souls who came to his table, patients whose roots were weak, who had little sunshine and nourishment in their lives, often through no fault of their own.

What am I doing it all for? His parents had raised him to be strong, moral and determined. To succeed. And he had. He was blessed. But what was true success? What really mattered in the short life he had to live? Ben squeezed the steering wheel. Showing everyone that the critics hadn't won? That the bullies hadn't succeeded in holding him down? And, perhaps, that McKenzie Price hadn't broken his heart?

Kudzu Creek hadn't failed him, Ben realized. He'd been wrong to let anyone make him feel ashamed for having a loving and secure family and for wanting an admirable career. He'd let a few bad apples poison his outlook on life and his hometown. He'd never thought he could be friends again with McKenzie—but he'd been wrong about that.

Fields of dry, cold soil streamed by the window, and Ben missed the summer days of his youth. In July, Kudzu Creek was a green, golden world with honeysuckle and kudzu vines, trickling brown streams, red dusty clay, and constellations that lit up the sky brighter than any city lights. A warm, soothing sensation flooded through his veins. He thought of home often, his parent's house, jolly Creek Street, and long, curling roads with fields of peanuts and melons that sprang to life in the spring. But most of all, in his quietest moments, he thought of McKenzie—the little girl who'd held his hand on the playground and took turns on the swings. The one who walked him to the library when he had no one to eat lunch with, who introduced him to *Treasure Island* and the Hardy Boys. She was the young woman who had bolstered his confidence when his grades were less than perfect; who had shrugged off the teasing about his hair, his father, his love of music and the pleasure he took in the band. She'd stood beside him their entire childhood until he asked for more…after which, he hardened a part of his heart. Against her. Against them all.

Respect. Is that what he'd been chasing all this time, or had it been some form of egotistical revenge? Were his dreams driven more by vanity than out of a desire to serve? Ben stared through the windshield, his chest heavy.

Maybe McKenzie was right: maybe he'd left Georgia because he wanted to prove something. That was what the car was about, anyway. The clothes. The watch. They hadn't accepted him, so he'd left to show them he didn't need his father, that he could make it on his own, and that he could be more successful and admired than anyone else—a hero instead of a zero. A star instead of a feeble candle in a window.

Ben grimaced. Well, he'd succeeded, and what did he have to show for it? No real address, no woman by his side, few friends and a child who treated him like a casual acquaintance. And Megan preferred her grandpa's old pickup truck to his flashy car. Ben inhaled as he braked for the driveway that started after he passed the tall metal mailbox dressed in holly and ivy with his family name emblazoned across the side. There was less than a month left until he returned to Chicago. Maybe Megan would be a little sad to see him go. Maybe they could forge a bond that distance could not destroy. Maybe someday, he could be the father she deserved.

Chapter Ten

McKenzie strolled through the back door of the diner, inhaling cleaner and fry grease. It brought an odd sort of comfort. She looked around the dim kitchen. The cooks had not clocked in. By the light in the office, she suspected Mayer had arrived and was crunching numbers on the computer at his new desk. She wondered if he slept at Southern Fried Kudzu. He did nothing but manage the business, other people and himself. Did he ever pick up a book? She smiled to herself and headed for the flour bin. By the time she was on her third batch of biscuits, Barney had clomped in, wearing his favorite greasy black loafers. She wished him a good morning, and they chatted about his grandson, who was starting an online newspaper for his school. "A good use of technology," she joked as she checked the new digital clock over the fryers. The old one had been coated with years of grime, but it ticked; the new replacement blinked, had an alarm, changed colors and, unfortunately, shut off when steam from the fryers clogged up its system.

With a shrug, McKenzie trotted out to the dining room and unlocked the front door. She breezed back to the counter to start the coffee, then remembered everyone's favorite brand was gone. She stared with displeasure at the espresso machine that someone had already started to get the boilers hot. Frowning, she checked the bakery display and found it not only dirty but with two half-empty trays inside. The tarts and muffins would be dried out or worse. She sighed and began to clean up, but before she could refill it with pastries from the freezer, the first customers of the day wandered in. She quickly put aside her frustrations to welcome them in because they mattered more.

Three hours later, she wiped down the last empty table and returned to the back of the diner for a break. The new cook, Terry, had arrived, and she greeted him with a friendly hello after telling Barney goodbye. He'd tipped a red baseball cap, then departed, leaving her on a stool at the counter. Angela took over the front while McKenzie munched on a sandwich Barney had made for her and looked at her phone to check the schedule. It had not changed overnight—she only had two hours left rather than her usual four to six. McKenzie wondered if she should go by the clinic and ask Ben if he wanted her to pick up Megan regularly. It was the least she could do. She knew he was busy with his father's caseload. On Sunday after church, he'd told her he had a new patient on the weekend, a woman who'd first refused to see him when he came into town. She smiled. No one could ever accuse Ben of holding grudges—he was a good Christian and a better man for it. He was even on call on weekends. Yes, she mused, setting down her lunch and reaching for a napkin, the boy she'd admired had become a good man. Someday, someone would cherish him and give him everything he deserved. Her heart tweaked with an unexpected pinch of envy. If only she hadn't been so afraid to take the next step so many years ago—that someone could have been her. But he'd moved on. He even had a child. McKenzie thought of Megan, and her heart hurt as she wondered what it would have been like if she had been the little girl's mother.

"Miss Price." A nasally voice interrupted her wistfulness.

McKenzie wiped her mouth and balled up her napkin. "I was just on my lunch break early," she told Mayer as she slid off the stool. She scanned the kitchen and saw Terry had everything under control. "Where would you like me?"

"In my office." Mayer turned on his heel.

She would have rolled her eyes for Barney's benefit, but he wasn't there, so the foggy digital clock had to do. Making an effort to be patient, McKenzie followed Mr. Mayer into the tiny office and stood behind a chair across from his desk.

"Please sit down," he said after taking his seat.

She glanced toward the door, glad she'd left it open. "I can stand," McKenzie insisted, "unless this is going to take long." The bell on the front door jangled again.

"Very well," said Mr. Mayer in a stiff tone. Voices echoed from the dining room.

"Mr. Mayer, I should probably get back outside and help Angela."

"Angela is fine," said Mayer.

"Order number forty-seven," cracked an unsteady voice over the staticky intercom.

"She doesn't like the microphone," McKenzie informed him. He stared at her, his face a curious blank expression. He was as bland as the can of salt substitute hardening in the diner's pantry. McKenzie shifted uncomfortably, wondering if she'd overstepped. It was just that Mayer did not seem aware of how the other employees felt any more than he did the customers. He just saw columns, numbers and bottom lines.

"Miss Price," he began at last, "there's no reason for you to stay the last two hours of your shift."

McKenzie raised her brows, frustrated. "Five hours is a short shift, and the kitchen's already expecting me to be here so Angela isn't on her own."

Mayer cleared his throat, and McKenzie braced herself. "As I tell you, often," he interjected, "I will be here to assist any employee who finds himself or herself in need. You may go, and…" He hesitated, and to her surprise, a splotch of color formed on both cheeks, making his dull brown eyes brighten. "There is no reason for you to return tomorrow. Or Friday. Or next week."

McKenzie's mind was busy calculating her next small check, but it came to a screeching halt. It felt like the air had been siphoned from the room, leaving it hot and stuffy. "I'm sorry. What?" Something deep in her eardrums burned.

Mayer unclasped his hands and leaned back in his chair, making it rock. He almost looked smug. "You may not know," he explained, "but I promised my uncle I would take his revenues and double them by the end of the year."

"That's v-very ambitious," stammered McKenzie, although she hadn't known the details. The revenues were increasing long before Mayer had arrived. She suddenly wished she'd sat down in the chair after all when her stomach clenched in warning.

"After going through the numbers," said Mayer, nodding toward his computer, "there is no need to have three employees when two will do."

McKenzie gripped the chair with her fingertips. "I don't understand."

"You make higher wages than anyone else at the diner."

"I've been here almost as long as Barney, and I've managed it for years," she explained, trying to keep her voice from trembling.

"Unofficially," Mayer corrected her. "Technically, you were only supervising, but now that we are under new management..." He coughed, then continued, "Well, as you must know, I can hire two workers at a minimum wage to do all that you do."

McKenzie's heart spasmed. "No one can do what I do," she said defensively. "Except maybe Mrs. Hill. It's her recipe, the tarts. She's the one who taught me how to bake biscuits, too."

Mayer shrugged. "There is nothing to making a biscuit. You can buy them frozen these days, and they taste just as good."

"But they're not homemade!" blurted out McKenzie.

"That's neither here nor there," returned the man behind the desk. He rocked again, and the chair creaked. They stared at each other, and McKenzie hated herself for the beseeching look she knew was in her eyes. She could guess what he was going to say before he said it.

"I'm afraid I must let you go," he said , rocking gently. "With excellent references, of course." He sighed as if it pained him to say so. "Although you are rather bullheaded about change."

"I am not!" McKenzie exclaimed, trying to turn her shock into outrage. "I've been at the diner since I was sixteen years old."

"Precisely," agreed Mayer, as if she were an antique. "But change is necessary for growth— for this diner." He leaned forward. "I'm sure you understand."

"So…" McKenzie's thoughts wrestled in her head. "You want me to leave?"

"Yes, now." Mayer smiled. "I can handle things from here."

"But what about—"

"Now, please." Mayer's polite expression became as dry as old plaster.

Her mind raced. "Shouldn't I wait a couple weeks to train someone?" *Isn't there a severance plan?* McKenzie thought desperately. They couldn't fire her! She was McKenzie Price. The keeper of the tart recipe. The morning's biscuit-maker. The coffee-starter, the menu-explainer, and the cleanup crew for the dining room and public restroom.

Mayer's eyes returned to their dull, fish-eyed calm. "No, Miss Price. Nothing more is required of you. Please come by Monday for a reference from me if you would like one." He sounded as if he was trying to be kind, but McKenzie felt the world spinning. Her eyes darted around the room, where she'd taken breaks, read so many books, eaten hundreds of Barney's delicious sandwiches, laughed with her coworkers and cried with some, too. With panic squeezing her chest like a lemon press, she dashed from the room, grabbed her purse and escaped to her car. She peeled out of the alley and onto Creek Street before spinning the steering wheel in the opposite direction of her home. Clutching the wheel with her hands, she held back tears until she hit the town limits.

Thank You for Coming. Come Back Soon.

The little sign that marked the boundary of Kudzu Creek unleashed her emotions. She burst into tears, sobbing quietly as she drove along a narrow highway lined with skinny pines and thick trees wearing the remnants of autumn. Sniffling with despair, she noticed a sign for a trail down to the creek—a swimming hole in Kudzu Creek she'd used through the years that would now be running thin and cold while kudzu withered on its banks. She turned and eased the car into a gravel parking spot but remained in the car to wipe her face after fumbling through the glove box for tissues. She had to pull herself together. She had no one besides Jill—her busy, struggling sister—to turn to for advice and help. She couldn't do that, though. She needed to be Jill's rock. Wasn't there anyone?

McKenzie stared through the windshield at the meandering creek. She'd never realized how much she kept people at arm's length. She had her sweet ladies from the book club, acquaintances at church and a few friends from her childhood, but none of them were people she could open up to about the hard stuff. No one she could confide in about her pain. With a wince, McKenzie admitted she didn't let anyone get too close. At one time in her life, she'd even pushed Ben away. A breath hitched in her throat. Believing that Jill would never move somewhere else if she did all she could to support her was as silly as not letting anyone in her personal life because they might leave, too. How could she find the one she was meant to share her life with if she kept dismissing anyone who did not bury his boots in the red clay of Kudzu Creek? Was she missing out on blessings by staying in the town that had always been there for her?

A pale reflection of herself stared back pitifully from the rearview mirror. What if the diner had never been God's plan? What if the job she'd put her heart and soul into was not where she was supposed to be right now? What if she'd been wrong about everything she thought was right? She considered her childhood. She'd wanted to be an archaeologist. A school teacher. She'd even thought about becoming a librarian—but the thing that made her heart soar the most was the idea of sitting, day after day, in her very own shop, surrounded by packed bookshelves that smelled like well-traveled paper and tea and coffee.

The old secret wish picked up speed, and McKenzie turned back to the view of the creek. A life with books and a tight, loving family. The desire hadn't disappeared—she'd just pushed it to the corners of her heart and filed it away under *Dreams*. And yet… For years she had convinced herself they were all impossible fantasies, just as Ben had said. She looked at herself in the mirror. The skin around her eyes was beginning to develop fine lines that radiated out from the corners. Ben had dreamed a dream, and like a hunting dog on the scent, he'd put his head down and gone to work, not worrying about what would happen if he failed.

She'd worked, she told herself, but for what? Her business classes had prepared her to own a business someday, and buying the diner had not only been the most sensible and perfect route, but it'd also been the easiest and the safest, too. McKenzie allowed a long, tired exhale. The odds of Mr. Hill selling her the diner now that she'd been fired by his nephew were slim to none. The new manager could now decide he wanted to purchase it for himself, and perhaps he'd had that on his mind from the start and was eliminating anyone in his way. With a groan, McKenzie realized she was not as secure as she thought she was. She had no control over her life. Again. Her hand went to her chest, and she pressed down, grasping for faith in something to collect herself. Everyone she loved was still breathing, she told herself. And so was she.

Ben could hardly wait to pick Megan up from school and drive her to dance class. She'd begun to talk a little about her school day without prodding, and she said goodbye to him after hopping out of the car. She even looked over her shoulder and waved. "Things are going well," he assured his dad when he stopped by the house to hand him the Dougherty file to look over.

"Did you hear from the hospital in Atlanta about Mr. Dougherty?"

"Yes." Ben sat on the couch beside his father, who'd regained color in his cheeks and most of his mobility. A documentary about Yellowstone, a place his father had wanted to visit for years, droned from the television across the room. "He was released after a few days, but he did make it back to the specialist there."

"He could have had a stroke."

"Yes, a major one. It might have left him paralyzed or worse."

Dad shook his head. "I've been after him for years to change his diet, but some people just won't listen."

"I know," said Ben. "It can be frustrating." He said nothing about Mom's biscuits and gravy again.

Megan wandered into the room and sat on the floor in front of the television with two dolls. "It's not too different from raising children," Dad said with a sigh.

"Is that right?" Ben couldn't imagine Megan being stubborn or defiant, but he knew enough about child development that those days were on the horizon. He sat back, thinking about his father's observation. "You never found me too obstinate to listen, did you?"

"We were blessed—you went above and beyond." Dad winked at him. "Most of the time."

"What do you mean?"

Dad reached for a deck of cards and dealt a hand between them. "Let's play before you have to rush off to your dance lesson."

Ben smirked. "I think I may be more coordinated than I used to be, and that's just from watching." They played a few hands while the geysers encircled by snow in Yellowstone erupted on the television.

"What I meant was," said Dad without looking up, "sometimes you didn't take the hint if I didn't come right out and make the suggestions."

"Like what?" His father glanced at Megan in front of the TV. Ben's chest tightened. "I know you thought I got married too fast."

"The first time," his father admitted.

"What do you mean the first time? There hasn't been a second."

"Not yet, but I hope there will be."

Ben remembered what McKenzie had told him about his little girl. "I know Megan needs a mother," he said. "A real one. Someone present."

"She needs a father, too."

Ben ducked his head to focus on the card game. He stared at the hand he'd been dealt. "I was young and busy, distracted…"

"But now?"

"Now things are different," said Ben. "I can visit more. I'll be there for her." His father didn't look satisfied. "I'm going to miss her," Ben contended. His throat caught. "I'll miss her so much that I'll probably call her every day."

After a few minutes of silent of card play, Dad said, "She'll like that."

When McKenzie let Bailey out of the car to walk inside Miss Sherry's, she caught herself checking her hair in the mirror for too long. She wanted to make sure she looked okay. It wasn't Ben, she told herself. And it wasn't that she'd noticed his car in the parking lot. It was because after moping for a whole day, she'd decided to have her hair cut and styled as well as get a manicure after Jill's urging to do something for herself and not worry about the future. The shorter hairstyle did make her feel better, but it didn't resolve her concerns about finding new employment.

She'd cleaned the house from top to bottom, washed everyone's sweaters by hand, and raked leaves until she gave up and blew them away into the woods with a leaf blower, wishing her problems would blow away, too. McKenzie studied her lip gloss, decided she looked presentable and let herself out of the car, wondering how many people had heard she was no longer at the diner. Several heads turned when she walked in, and she tried not to gulp. Claire nodded, and she gave her a small wave. Ben smiled from their usual spot on the bleachers, and McKenzie strolled over as if her heart was not jumping with relief at the sight of him. It also did a yearning swan dance, which she dismissed. She was just happy to see someone who cared about her.

"You didn't bring the catering order in this week," he said in a disappointed tone when she sat down.

She looked at him in surprise. "You haven't heard."

"Heard what?"

McKenzie looked around the room anxiously to see if anyone was in earshot. Claire hadn't stayed. "Who brought it in?"

"Some kid. Said he was new. The sandwiches were good, though."

"Were they? I'm glad." McKenzie watched Miss Sherry gather the students to begin stretching. She smiled when Megan caught her eye. The little girl grinned and waved back.

"Are you okay?"

"Sure."

"You look nice."

McKenzie tingled at the compliment. No one had said that in a long time—not that she'd ever put in any effort in that department. It was silly to start now, but then again, she did have the time for it. "Thanks. How's Megan?"

"She's doing okay. I showed her how to start a video chat on my dad's tablet. It's amazing how fast children learn."

"It's a new generation," McKenzie mused. Yes, everyone seemed able to conquer new things these days but her. She cleared her throat, inhaling Ben's romantic-stroll-under-the-pines scent. It comforted her. She wanted to scoot closer and lean her head on his shoulder, but that might give him the wrong idea.

"Are you sure you're okay?" He gave her a side-eye. "Do you have a date and you're afraid to tell me about it?" A laugh gurgled in her throat and escaped as McKenzie searched his eyes. "I won't get jealous. I promise." He seemed sincere, and he'd gotten over her once—if he meant everything he professed so many years before. It seemed like a lifetime ago. A lifetime she'd missed out on.

McKenzie looked away and watched the reflection of the couple in the mirror across the room. A handsome man was watching her with concern etched into his face. The striking man was Ben. "I...uh," she began in a low tone. Squaring her shoulders, she turned to face him with a breath of defiance. It was a small town. Everyone would know eventually. "I was let go at the diner on Wednesday. The new look is for my job hunt."

"What?" Ben's forehead creased with lines of confusion.

"I got fired. Sacked. Canned," she elaborated, trying to be funny.

He stared in shock. "You're kidding."

McKenzie pasted on a look of nonchalance. "Nope. Mr. Mayer informed me he could hire two workers to replace me for the same cost, and so he did. No thank-you. No goodbye. No time to look for something else."

"But—"

She held up her hand without looking. "It's fine. You said so yourself—it's time to try something new."

"I never hoped that would happen..." Ben faltered.

McKenzie set her elbows on her knees. "Do you know any good restaurants in need of a good tart-maker? Biscuit-starter? Bathroom janitor?" He stared silently. "No? Me either."

"I'm sorry, McKenzie," said Ben softly. "That's not fair."

The children began line dancing to a Garth Brooks' Christmas rendition of *Winter Wonderland*. Ignoring Ben's pity, McKenzie began to clap along. He followed her lead, and eventually, so did the other parents. Everyone cheered when it ended, and Miss Sherry called for the students to circle around her. She sat on the floor and splayed out her leg warmers.

"I have a wonderful and exciting announcement!" Over her shoulder, she added, "Parents, this is something you need to know."

Ben reached for McKenzie's hand and pulled her up. "We may want to hear this." She felt a rush of connection when his fingers curled around hers, and she held on for as long as she could until he let go. She gawked at Miss Sherry like she was concentrating on her every word.

"There's going to be an addition to our Christmas dance recital," she announced. "We are going to have the fathers dance too."

The children *ooh*ed, and to McKenzie's utter astonishment, Megan looked up and called out, "Oh, Daddy!" with glee.

"Oh yes," said Miss Sherry, shooting Ben a smirk. "It will be a daddy–daughter dance." She stopped at Leo Ainsworth's cry of protest. "And a daddy–son dance, too." The little boy crossed his arms but lowered his brows, mollified.

McKenzie laughed and elbowed Ben. "You get to dance after all." For some reason, she had to blink back tears. "And with your daughter." Her mind raced. Had she ever danced with her father? No, and she'd never wanted to, either. *Megan is blessed,* she thought sadly. Did Ben even know how fortunate he was to have someone that belonged to him?

Megan had already returned to chatting with her friends, but Ben made a soft noise under his breath. It sounded like he couldn't breathe. McKenzie realized he looked pale. "Bailey, I'll be outside," she called out as the children climbed to their feet to practice their last dance routine. She grabbed Ben by the wrist and pulled him out of the dance studio with her.

Once in the parking lot, she let go of him so he wouldn't suspect that tumultuous feelings brewed inside her gut whenever she touched him. She tried to smother them, reminding herself that a true friend would get to the bottom of things and listen, not obsess over, holding hands. She led him to her car, then spun around and put her fists on her waist. A chilly breeze whisked around them, carrying the pleasant scent of burning brush in the distance. "Okay. What gives? You practically turned gray in there."

Ben stared back with a slack jaw. He gulped. "A dance recital? Me?"

"It will only be one dance."

"But I can't dance."

"Take your French horn."

He shook his head.

"Mellophone?"

"Seriously, Mac, I can't do it."

McKenzie reared back in surprise. "Yes, you can, Ben. I've danced with you in gym class for years and last month in the studio." She pointed a finger at him. "You aren't just a brain, Ben Cooper. You can dance, too."

He made a face like he'd slurped a spoonful of castor oil. "I can't."

"When you set your mind to it and stop worrying about whether other people think it's perfect or not, you can."

"What if I make a fool of myself?" he groaned.

"I doubt Scotty or Billy will show up," McKenzie assured him. "And who cares?"

"But—"

"I don't understand you," blustered McKenzie. "You asked me to go to college with you in front of the whole band—"

"So?" he interrupted.

"That took a lot of nerve. You opened yourself up to rejection, jeers."

"And you rejected me," he blurted out. There was no bitterness in his tone, no blame, but McKenzie wondered if she heard something else, a morsel of lingering regret—the same regret that'd been suffocating her since he'd come back to town.

They stared at each other, and his eyes became dark and deep. There were red highlights in his lashes, and it took McKenzie back to the flashing tangerine-brown hair of his childhood. It'd been a beautiful, earthy shade that reminded her of red-gold summer sunsets. His colors, inside and out, made her happy. Made her smile. Like the cardinal flowers that grew along the roadside in the summer, he'd flowered into a striking specimen—quiet but rugged, with wider shoulders, a thicker throat and a neckline that made her want to brush her fingers along its outline. This made her happy, too, and strangely achy. She swallowed and looked away.

"It was my fault, Ben," McKenzie whispered. "I was scared. You were my best friend, and I didn't want to lose that. You saw what happened with the other couples at school after they went to college—the fights, the breakups, the not speaking to one another anymore. Even families got involved. And then there were my parents. They weren't kind to each other, but I knew they loved each other once upon a time. But it turned to bitterness. Hatred. Sometimes aggression. It was so confusing for me. Friendship just seemed safer all around."

Ben listened quietly. "I didn't know how badly you were affected by all that. I knew you struggled—that you and your sister were alone—two birds in a hurricane. I should have considered how you'd feel about me asking you to go to college with me out of the blue—changing what we had—before you had time to think about it." He shook his head. "I shouldn't have done it. I'm sorry."

"No, don't be. You were just trying to be kind and be there for me. To get me out of this town."

"And to tell you that I loved you," he added. They both froze, and Ben's face reddened. "I wasn't afraid to leave, but I wanted you to go with me. You were my support system. I didn't think I could do it without you."

"But you did."

"Yes, I survived." He studied her. "Only because I had no choice. I called home a lot."

"I was afraid, too," McKenzie insisted. "I knew you were leaving. I had no one to be there for me after Jill got married if I didn't make it. So I told myself it was time to pull away. Now that I think about it, asking me to leave with you was the perfect opportunity." She looked up at him from under her lashes. "Don't think I didn't cry my share of tears."

"Really?"

"Really."

"Well, I survived," admitted Ben. "Even with a little teasing from Scotty and Billy. Especially when we didn't show up at prom together."

"I'm surprised they noticed."

He shrugged. "I didn't go. I'm sure they were there, looking for someone to harass."

McKenzie cocked her head. "I didn't know that. Me either."

"I figured you'd go with someone else."

"I didn't." They smiled at each other. McKenzie resisted the urge to jab her finger in his chest. "What silly kids we were back then. But you did leave without saying goodbye."

Ben winced. "It just seemed easier. I'm sorry. I didn't think about how your mom did that to you, too. I had a crushed ego and a bruised heart."

"I guess I did, too." Something told McKenzie she'd ignored a wound that had never healed, a hole she'd never admitted she had. "I h-hope you were happy with Chetana," she stammered. She was the girl who'd truly won Ben's heart.

"We were, for a time."

"I'm sure you'll be happy again."

Ben gave McKenzie a tight smile. "I guess so, but for now," he murmured, "I have a little girl that needs me, and I need to be more than a doctor. More than a son. I need to be a father."

Happiness for Megan seemed to rain down from the cloudy sky. "That's wonderful, Ben," McKenzie whispered. "You succeeded. That's why this town loves and admires you. I know Megan will be fine because she has a father who is a great man and loves her."

He gave a curt nod. "Yes, well, in only a few weeks, I head back, so I hope you'll still feel that way after I go." He shuffled his feet. "I know you think I should stay, but she's happy here. She'll be okay."

"I know she'd be happy if she was with you, too," McKenzie assured him. *I would have been,* her heart whispered.

It was as if he'd heard her thought. They locked gazes. Standing so close to him, McKenzie could see the curve of his bottom lip and feel his gaze wandering over her face, giving her goose bumps. He'd never looked at her like that before, and she liked it.

As if they were two magnets, Ben leaned in, and she met him halfway, as his lips brushed over hers. She looped her arms around his neck, and pulled herself into a warmth and protection she never expected. She was hardly aware of the chill cutting through her sweater or the echo of little voices in her head.

The children.

McKenzie jerked back, breaking their connection with regret. She realized her pulse was at full gallop, and Ben's cheeks looked as dark as beets. "I'm sorry," he blurted out.

"I'm f-fine," she stammered. *He was sorry?* She spun around as Bailey came skipping up.

"What are you doing, Aunt McKenzie?"

"We're not doing anything," McKenzie said in a rush. "I mean, *I'm* not doing anything." She forced a smile that felt plastic. "Just waiting." She couldn't bear to look at Ben again. It was unintentional—they'd been standing too close, talking about old days. Her feelings about the past and the new Ben Cooper were all mixed up. "It was nothing," she repeated. "Nothing at all." Ben nodded vehemently in agreement, and his enthusiasm at her assertion stabbed McKenzie right in the chest.

Chapter Eleven

Saturday afternoon, after lunch and chores, Megan mentioned wanting to have another sleepover with Bailey, and Ben thought he might be sick. After all they'd rehashed and resolved, he'd been stupid enough to get sucked into McKenzie's beautiful gaze the night before and kiss her. It was everything he'd always dreamed of—a bolt of lightning had blasted his soul wide open while his feelings spun into a tornado of joy—but it was all for nothing. She'd said so. Reality had crashed into him like a cannonball. He'd hardly been able to drive home and stayed awake all night—sleep eluding him.

What was he doing? He had promised himself he wouldn't fall for her again. He had to protect his heart—and their fragile friendship. A second mistake with McKenzie might ruin him…and he'd likely never take a chance with anyone else.

Luckily, it was too far into the weekend to issue a last-minute invitation, so on a whim, he dug out two sleeping bags from his closet and spread them out beside the Christmas tree in the living room, inviting Megan to camp out. She beamed with excitement, and they spent hours underneath the tree, discussing her Christmas list. As his daughter grew drowsy and drifted off to sleep beside him on the floor, her soft breath filled his life with an innocence he never thought he'd feel again. He looked up at the colorful lights dancing in the boughs.

He saw it now: Megan was the guiding light he'd been missing. Ever since he'd moved away, slogged through his education and ruined his relationship with her mother, he felt like a soul lost in space—a hurtling comet with no home keeping him on a steady path to lead him to where he belonged. Even his successes had not filled the hole. Megan was what he needed in his life, what mattered, and she'd been here, in Kudzu Creek, all along.

The weight sitting on his chest eased as Ben realized he could go back to Chicago with a whole new sense of peace. He was a father.

They had a connection. He would be there for her. And someday, they would be a real family.

He heard his parents' bedroom door open down the hall, then Mom's footsteps, Ben crawled up to get a drink of water before sneaking into his own bed. He was getting too old to sleep on the floor, he thought wistfully. Leaving the kitchen, he noticed a small light coming from underneath his parents' door. He knocked gently, and when his father called to come in, he walked in to find him staring at the ceiling with a book in his lap.

"Dad? Are you okay?"

His father picked up his book as if he'd been caught woolgathering. "Yes, I'm just trying to finish this."

Ben sat down beside him in a chair by the nightstand. "What's it about?"

"The Cherokee Blood Wars. Interesting reading. Humbling. Sad…"

Ben thought of McKenzie. "I didn't know you liked history that much."

"From our neck of the woods, the south. I've just never had time to do a whole lot of reading until now."

"I'm glad you have the opportunity."

Dad met Ben's casual gaze, his blue eyes

full of a depth that indicated he had more on his mind than history.

"What's wrong, Dad?"

His father smiled. "I've had a lot to think about."

"Things at the clinic are fine," Ben assured him. "You know there were a few patients who refused to see me, but I think they'll come back when you get back to work."

"That's what's on my mind," said Dad.

Ben's heart sank. Had he failed his father, too? His father patted his chest. "This may have been a sign. I think it's time for a new chapter in my life that doesn't include the clinic."

Ben's brain misfired like an electrical connection had popped. "No." He felt his brow furrow. "You can't retire."

"Why not?"

"Because you have so many years left."

"Of work?" Dad laughed. "I know I'm lucky to be here, and I'm not that old yet—but why wait until I can't enjoy retirement to actually do it?" He looked around the room. "Besides, I've been promising your mother that we'd update the house for years and travel some, too."

"With Megan?"

Dad looked at Ben pointedly. "I guess we

need to talk about that. Someday, things are going to have to change."

Ben sat back in the chair. "You're right, but it's going to be hard on all of us."

His father pulled off his reading glasses and folded them carefully before setting them on the nightstand. "You know big decisions are hard. Sometimes we have to take a step into the darkness, trusting God knows where to set our feet."

"I understand that," Ben assured him. "It was hard for me to leave Kudzu Creek. Hard to live in a college town on my own, then move across the country to medical school." He exhaled. "Even Chicago was hard, but I learned to love it. It's a great place. There're good people there, just like here."

"I'm glad you're happy there," his dad agreed, "but do you know what's next? Who's next? Have you heard about a fellowship?"

"Not yet," Ben admitted.

"Is that where you think you belong?"

"I never really think about where I belong," Ben admitted. "I'm just trying to get the training I need." He hesitated, mind whirling. Or was it the praise? The accolades? Had his childhood monsters turned him into a Napoleon? "Dad, what about the clinic? If you retire, what'll happen to Darlene and Mindy? And your patients, too? Ms. Olivia can't get very far without a cane. And then there's Mr. Dougherty. He'll need follow-ups."

Dad gave Ben a soft smile. "Albany isn't that far of a drive, and we do have a health department here."

"What about the clinic's building?"

"I just lease it. I'm sure someone else will snap it up. The town's having a growth spurt."

"Yes, I know. A lot has changed around here." Ben didn't mean Creek Street, he realized, or even the old coffee shop that was now a diner. People had grown, too—most of them, for the better. He smiled faintly at his father. "I hope you have a long reading list."

"I don't suppose I can talk you into taking over the clinic?" His dad never did beat around the bush. "I think it'd be good for you to be home."

The idea was laughable. Ben would never thrive in Kudzu Creek, despite the fact that he saw it through different lenses now. He'd never become the head of a surgical department. And, he admitted, he'd never be able to keep thinking of McKenzie as his friend, not forever, not after the way he'd kissed her. Not after the way she'd kissed him back. "No," he said sadly, and it felt like his chest sank to his knees.

"Not even for a second chance with someone special?" hinted his father.

Ben's cheeks warmed. "I'm going to assume y-you're talking about my daughter," he stammered, "and we're working on that. Anyone else, well—there's no one here I'd have a chance with, just a few special friends."

McKenzie picked up Bailey from school and drove straight to Alabaster's in response to a message from Diane, hoping against hope she wouldn't run into Mr. Mayer. She'd filled out an application for a bakery in the next town over and looked at the county library's job openings online, but nothing felt right. She was hardly sleeping, either, with strange dreams of kissing Ben in the middle of a creek while kudzu knotted around her legs. And then there were nightmares of Mayer calling out orders from the dining room faster than she could deliver them. Every time she shut her eyes, she was falling or failing, and she felt the same way when she opened them.

She pulled up to Alabaster's, trying not to look up and down the street to see if anyone noticed her. Just driving into town made her chest tighten. She'd avoided church the day before and felt guilty, but part of her felt like she'd been kicked out of society since being fired from Southern Fried Kudzu. "Let's go," she murmured to Bailey as she slid out of the car.

"Okay. Can we buy a candle that smells like gingerbread?"

Bailey was in full holiday mode. She skipped ahead, delighted with the snowflakes painted on the store's windows, and McKenzie tried to absorb some of her enthusiasm. They found a few lingering customers inside, with Diane at the register, staring at a computer printout. McKenzie sniffed a lungful of apple and cinnamon fragrances, and it instantly relaxed her. Even in the worst of times, there was something special about Christmas. She'd been wrong to think there'd be no joy.

"Hi, Ms. Diane. I like your snowflakes!" Bailey called. When Diane looked up, McKenzie waved.

"Thank you, little miss," she replied, smiling at Bailey. She glanced at McKenzie. "Bailey, if you go to the back and sneak down the hall, I have a bowl of chocolate candy hidden on the tall, white cabinet with Christmas tree angels."

"I love chocolate," cried Bailey. She hurried away.

Diane turned to McKenzie. "Oh, honey, I just heard this morning." She beckoned for her to join her at the counter and pulled out a stool. "Please, sit down a minute."

McKenzie braced herself. "You heard about the diner."

"How've you been?"

"I'm okay."

Diane studied her, and her concern made McKenzie's eyes well up and almost spill over.

"I am fine," she insisted, forcing a laugh. "I'm getting a lot done at home."

"You've worked at Southern Fried Kudzu for as long as anyone can remember," Diane mused.

"Then I guess it was time for me to go," McKenzie choked out.

"If you say so, but that's why I asked you to come by as soon as possible. I need help stocking shelves to keep up with the holidays. Especially the week before Christmas. Would you be interested?"

McKenzie flooded with relief at the temporary fix. "Can I let you know as soon as I'm able to work things out with Jill?"

"Sure thing, honey." Diane put a hand on her arm. "I don't suppose you heard about the uproar yesterday?"

"No, what happened?"

"They quit carrying Ms. Olivia's sweet tea next door."

McKenzie's mouth dropped open in horror. "What? Who doesn't sell iced tea?"

"They have it, but he changed sweeteners," Diane explained. "Something natural or trendy like that."

"Sugar's natural," moaned McKenzie. She leaned forward. "What'd Ms. Olivia do?"

"She asked to speak to the manager, told him the food had gone downhill and that the service was terrible!"

McKenzie sat back with satisfaction and crossed her arms. "That's very loyal of her."

"It was," Diane said with a sigh, "but I don't know if Mr. Mayer will take the hint. I know change is good and he's all about *progress, progress, progress*, but changing the menu that makes Southern Fried Kudzu what it is isn't a smart decision, if you ask me." She wrinkled her nose. "The hot dogs aren't even like the ball park's anymore."

"I think he ordered some plant-based weenies. He wants us to catch up with the times."

Diane hooted. "Honey, this is Georgia. We talk slow, eat slow and never make a decision before noon."

McKenzie smiled. "He was hired to double Mr. Hill's money, but it doesn't look promising, unfortunately. Not in the long run."

"No." Diane shook her head. "It's too bad you can't open your own diner, Mac. You have a good head for business, and you know how to make people feel loved and happy."

McKenzie was flattered, but she knew another diner in Kudzu Creek wouldn't do. "I'm no Lindsey Ainsworth. She's made the Azalea Inn famous with her baking, and I could never compete." She considered the reality. "The diner is a second home to me, and I could picture myself there until I'm old and gray, but I'll just have to have faith that the Lord can see something I can't around the corner."

"Good for you!" Diane patted her knee. "And who knows what'll spring up on the other side of Alabaster's?"

McKenzie raised a brow with interest. "Next door?"

Diane clarified, "The construction company is changing addresses."

"Parker and Associates Construction is closing?" McKenzie exclaimed. "What about Bradley's job?"

"Oh, no, they're just moving down the road. They bought an old house across the street from the Azalea on Pebble Stretch Road, and they're going to turn it into a new office and showroom."

"That's nice," said McKenzie slowly. "I guess Kudzu Creek is catching up with the world."

"Spreading out, anyway," said Diane. "But we still like our food fried and *real* weenies." She leaned close and lowered her voice after a glimpse at the customers wandering around the room. "I'm thinking about expanding," she confessed, "although I know I already have my hands full."

The front door swung open. McKenzie felt her heart do a *loop de loop* when Ben walked in with Megan at his side. He had a to-go bag from next door and froze mid-step when he saw her. "Oh, hi."

"Hi, Megan," she said in surprise.

"I came with Daddy to work today," said the little girl.

"How fun!" McKenzie shifted her gaze to Ben. He gave her a faint smile.

"Come on in, Dr. Cooper," Diane welcomed in a cheery voice. "What can I do for you today, or are you bringing me lunch?"

McKenzie could have sworn he blushed. "I was just grabbing something to eat and thought I'd see if I could find a history book for my dad from a local author."

"How's he doing?" asked Diane with sincerity.

"Much better." Ben strolled up to the counter with Megan at his heels. McKenzie braced herself as he said, "Hi, McKenzie. How're you?"

"I'm hanging in there," she offered, fighting a flush on her cheeks. Even though he'd only kissed her once, she felt a stab of betrayal that he'd been next door at Southern Fried Kudzu.

He caught her looking at his fast-food bag and shrugged helplessly. "They were supposed to cater next week but canceled on me."

"They aren't catering now?" McKenzie gasped.

"I guess business has been so good they decided we could pick up orders ourselves or cancel... And I went to tell them I decided to cancel."

"That's a shame," said Diane. She cast a meaningful glance over to McKenzie. "Told you it was going downhill without you there."

McKenzie let out a small chuckle. She noticed Megan staring at the small Christmas tree display with a porcelain nativity in the center of the room. "Would you like to look around the store?"

"Yes," she said sweetly. She made a beeline for the nativity, and her father followed her. With a quick glance at Diane, McKenzie went to join them, ignoring her watchful stare.

Ben smiled faintly when she stepped up beside him, and McKenzie pushed the kiss to the back of her mind. They were back to friendship. Back to normal. Whatever that meant. Neither one of them could just run away at this point.

"Look, Daddy!" Megan broke into a flurry of giggles. "That looks like Jiminy."

Ben chuckled. He picked up the ceramic donkey carefully, leaving the little family in the stable alone. "It sure does. He's watching over Baby Jesus."

"Some people believe there was a donkey in the stable that night," explained McKenzie. "Because in Isaiah, it says the donkey knows the master's manger."

Megan tilted her chin up and searched McKenzie's eyes. "He knew Jesus?"

"I'm sure he did," she promised. She felt Ben's stare and winked at him.

"He was watching over their family," said Megan. She turned back to the display and reached out to caress the top of Mary's head. "Jesus had a mommy and a daddy, too."

A knot rose in McKenzie's throat at the little girl's wistful tone. Unfortunately, it just didn't work out for everyone. Ben cleared his throat. "Have you found a new job?"

McKenzie stared at the nativity, steeling herself inside. "Not yet."

Diane joined their little party, startling her. "We're talking about having her come in to help out with Christmas stocking here," she said, beaming. "As soon as she's ready."

"I love your store, Ms. Diane," said Megan.

The woman smiled at her. "Thank you, sweetheart. Did you know Bailey was here? In the back. Why don't you go see what she's up to in my office?"

The little girl looked at Ben for permission, and when he nodded, she darted away. McKenzie breathed in what smelled like peace on earth, and she smiled. Megan was right. No other Help Wanted ads had tempted her, and at Alabaster's, she would be able to remain in town. "I'll have to see," she said, "but most likely." She turned to Diane. "I'll let you know by tomorrow evening." Diane grinned with the anticipation of a yes.

"Is there anything I can do, McKenzie?" Ben's warm eyes seemed to seep through the coat of courage she'd shrugged into to come into town.

Her lip trembled. "No, we'll be fine," McKenzie said resolutely. "I'm pulling my weight at the house for Jill right now."

"She's lucky to have you," Ben assured her.

Diane dashed over to a bookshelf and returned with a hardcover book. "How about this one for your dad, Doc?"

Ben hardly looked at it, instead choosing to study McKenzie. "It looks great."

Smiling with satisfaction, Diane hurried to the register to ring it up, and McKenzie and Ben followed. "You tell your daddy we miss him," she instructed Ben, then exhaled. "I need to get a refill on my migraine medication. With the holidays upon us, it's only a matter of time before I have a flare-up."

"Just bring it by," Ben offered.

"That's so nice of you."

She rang up his purchase, but Ben's attention stayed on McKenzie, and she warmed under it. "Will you be coming to dance class Friday?"

She couldn't help but smile at the nervousness in his voice. "I hear the daddies are learning the routine for the dance recital, so you can bet I won't miss it."

Ben's face flushed, and he groaned. "I'll see you later, then. I'll definitely need your support."

"The daddies are dancing?" repeated Diane with curious delight.

McKenzie turned to her with a giggle. "Yes,

it should be wonderful. I know Megan is excited."

Ben groaned. "I'll do my best."

"You'll be wonderful!" Diane predicted.

He winced, called for Megan and headed for the door. McKenzie watched them go, a smile blooming on her cheeks as he departed with his cold lunch and the book tucked under his arm. When she caught Diane looking at her, she tried to smother it, but the woman chuckled.

"I don't think I've ever seen you so comfortable with anyone before, McKenzie."

"Yes, well…" McKenzie fumbled for excuses. "Ben has his career and little girl, so his life is full."

"Is yours?" Diane returned without missing a beat.

McKenzie's eyes nearly watered again, but she blinked it away. "Not without a job to contribute my share at home, it's not," she said quietly.

"Careers aren't everything," Diane reminded her. "Full-time homemaking is a job. An important one. It's fulfilling for most of us."

"I know, but I *want* to help Jill with Bailey." McKenzie picked up a stapler and fiddled with it, unable to look her friend in the eyes.

"You need other people in your life, too."

"I know I need to start letting people past the friendship zone," McKenzie admitted, "but…"

"Sometimes all you need is a best friend," Diane supplied. "Love can surprise you."

"Yes, I know," McKenzie admitted, but she didn't say why. Her heart burned with a warm, comforting flame. Diane was right. Ben had surprised her, and maybe she needed him in her life if his kisses meant as much to her as her mind and heart insisted they did. But he was devoted to his life outside Kudzu Creek, and to be honest, her heart was safer when tending to family and people she could just call…friends.

Chapter Twelve

Ben hadn't seen Bailey as a patient for a while, and truthfully, he missed visiting with her and her mother—and her aunt. He'd been fortunate to see McKenzie the day before in the gift shop. He'd spotted her car parked along Creek Street near the diner and hurried inside—only to find she wasn't there. A quick duck into Alabaster's for a book for his dad had paid off, and he was able to chat with her and make sure they were okay after his foolish decision to kiss her. Despite feigning indifference, his heart had bobbed around as her bright eyes and flushed cheeks reminded him of how beautiful she'd become. After that, he'd been in a much better mood the rest of the day, even though the food from Southern Fried Kudzu was barely edible.

This morning, he prepared a lunch and, since

he was at it, made Megan's, too. She pulled a chair up beside him and giggled as he told her about peanut butter, mayonnaise and banana sandwiches. Then, out of the blue, she looked up and asked if she could have a sleepover again. Once more, Ben's mind snapped back to McKenzie and all she'd done for his daughter. Her kindness knew no bounds. He wished her love did, too.

He met with Ms. Olivia his first hour at the clinic and then saw two cases of sore throats that reminded him of the upcoming flu season. Before he could make a note to tell his father to get a flu shot, Darlene handed him another file, and Ben trotted to room number two while scanning it. *Dougherty*. He bit inside his lip and let himself in.

Old man Dougherty was hunkering on the stool instead of the examination table. He folded his arms when he saw Ben, but he didn't glare. "So your pop's not up and at 'em yet," he observed in a grumble.

"No, Mr. Dougherty. He still has a couple of weeks of recovery, then he'll be joining me."

The engraved lines in Mr. Dougherty's forehead deepened, and his upside-down smile sank to his chin. "You hanging around, then?"

"Not much longer," answered Ben brusquely.

He imagined some of his father's patients were counting the days.

"That's too bad. I ain't ever been to Chicago," said Mr. Dougherty. "Never had a reason to."

"It's an interesting city," Ben assured him. "I'm not sure how much longer I'll be there, but I plan to return for now." They went over a treatment plan, and to his surprise, Dougherty didn't argue about the dietary changes or Ben's admonition to quit chewing tobacco. "You don't have to give up everything in your life," Ben explained to him. "Just try to find better substitutions."

"I guess you're right," Mr. Dougherty groused. "I don't want to have to have heart surgery like your daddy."

"This is the time to improve your health," Ben warned him, "and, more importantly, to prevent a stroke." He checked Mr. Dougherty's prescription dosages and offered a hand. To his surprise, he got a handshake.

"It's a good thing you suggested I go to Atlanta," the man admitted as they walked out of the room together.

"Yes, good thing," chuckled Ben. He opened the door to the waiting room and waved him through. Scotty caught his attention when he stood up in the corner. Ben froze, unsure whether to ignore him or say hello, but his professional instincts kicked in and he gave him a polite nod. Mr. Dougherty lumbered straight for the exit, but his son hesitated. Before Ben could turn away, his old classmate strode over to him, and Ben wondered if he was going to say something cruel. They stood toe to toe, but Scotty looked past him as if he couldn't meet his eyes. He raised his chin. "Doctors in Atlanta said you saved my daddy's life. Thanks for that." His stance was hard, but his voice said otherwise.

Ben cleared his throat. "You're welcome."

"Sorry I gave you such a hard time…you know, back then."

The apology was so unexpected Ben replied, "No, it's fine," before he could think of anything else.

"No hard feelings?"

"It's in the past." Ben swallowed his anxiety, humbled by someone he never thought he could respect.

"Yeah, thanks." Scotty took a tentative step backward as if he'd just faced a tribunal. His face was stamped with crimson splotches. "My mom appreciates you a-and… Well, see you later," he stammered.

"Sure." Ben felt heat creep up his neck.

"You staying around here, then?"

"Not much longer. I have a job waiting in Chicago."

"Too bad," Scotty said.

They stared at each other, sheepish but older and wiser. Slowly, Ben stuck out his hand. If he could make peace with McKenzie, who'd broken his heart, he could make peace with Scotty Dougherty, who'd unwittingly broken his spirit in the tender years of his youth. Scotty shook it, his hand dry and calloused and hard. "Thanks again, and Merry Christmas."

"Merry Christmas." Ben let the door shut between them, knowing this chapter of his life was closed and any remaining damage would heal on its own as long as he left it alone. When he walked into Room Two with his mind racing, Ms. Olivia greeted him with, "It's about time! Look at my new walking stick. This one has a falcon's head."

Ben called McKenzie on Wednesday and asked if Bailey could join Megan for a sleepover on the weekend, then told her all about Scotty's peace offering at the doctor's office. She was happy for him. She offered to pick up Megan from school, but he declined, citing the need to spend more time with her with Christmas fast approaching and his imminent departure.

When he asked her if she'd be at the girls' dance class on Friday, she assured him she would be, even though she was working a few hours in the mornings now for Diane. She wanted to see Ben again. Only this time, she promised herself, she would not loiter in the parking lot and succumb to the temptation to kiss him.

After starting a load of laundry, McKenzie toted a newspaper to the kitchen table with her lunch and plopped down to scan any local job advertisements to distract her mind from Ben Cooper and his kisses. The thought of the lucky women who would be part of his life in Chicago made her a little jealous. She grimaced. What a mistake she'd made when she refused to take a chance with him. Even though she'd stayed in Kudzu Creek, she should have let her heart go and offer it despite the distance. She sighed but then remembered to count her blessings. He was part of her circles again. She wouldn't mess it up a second time. Like Jill and Bailey, he meant too much, and she was a happier person when he was in her life.

McKenzie found a mention in the newspaper that Parker and Associates was moving as she hummed to holiday songs echoing from the turntable in the living room. Diane had been right: the construction company next door to her shop was closing, and the building's owner was offering a new lease for the space that would be empty now. She wondered how much rent would cost for the small location—not that it mattered. For now, she worked part-time for Diane and was a full-time homemaker and babysitter. The front yard was immaculate, and she was rather proud of it. Dance class was tonight; she had that to look forward to, besides a new soup recipe. McKenzie enjoyed watching Bailey, but she liked sitting with Ben, talking about old and new times even more. The day before she'd bought a can of cheeseballs, wondering how they could sneak them into their mouths during dance class without getting caught. It'd be fun for a laugh, but she knew she couldn't suggest they take them outside—part of her didn't trust herself to be alone with him. There was no way to forget about his kisses in the parking lot under the dark, silvery sky.

Her heart pattered anxiously in her chest the whole way to school, and after picking Bailey up, they went for ice cream before Bailey changed clothes in the car. When they arrived at the studio, she bounced out and dashed inside. McKenzie took her time, only to feel a blast of disappointment when she walked in and saw Ben hadn't arrived yet.

She sat in their spot on the bleachers and watched clusters of dads standing around, talking in low tones, as girls and boys chased each other in circles. Finally, Miss Sherry flew out of her office, and with a clap of her hands, lined everyone up to stretch. Donovan and Bradley Ainsworth were there, good-naturedly ribbing each other when Megan darted in and took up her usual spot beside Bailey. Ben strode across the room late, his gaze already on her when McKenzie saw him. She was relieved he'd made it. Megan would need her dad up on that stage, and McKenzie wanted to see it.

"What are you doing, Dr. Cooper? You belong up here with everyone else today." Miss Sherry planted her knuckles on her hips. The class tittered as Ben gave McKenzie a reluctant smile and pivoted toward the back of the studio. The routine looked easy enough to pick up, and McKenzie chortled until her sides ached as the fathers shook their hips, trying to keep time with the music. Ben was much improved, but his efforts to stay in sync with Megan weren't enough, and the spectacle sent the little girl into hysterical giggles until he scooped her up in his arms, laughing. The sight of it melted McKenzie's heart. She could hardly imagine the love and support he would offer as a husband. Her stomach ballooned with butterflies, and she squeezed her sides to make them go away. She had to put these feelings to rest. Despite her talk with Diane, some things were just too risky to change. She could lose his friendship—and him—forever. And he was leaving, she reminded herself. He was not a constant in her life. She straightened and sent him a small smile when he looked in her direction, oblivious to her tangled thoughts.

Afterward, they met in the parking lot; Bailey had her overnight bag packed and ready to go. McKenzie ticked off instructions on her fingers. Her niece had pajamas, a toothbrush, a stuffed bear and a change of clothes for the next day. "Don't worry, we got it," Ben assured her. "And my mother will be there as well."

"We're having peanut butter and banana sandwiches," Megan announced, and Bailey wailed, "Gross!"

McKenzie laughed. "I'm sure you'll survive."

"There will be pizza on the side," vowed Ben. He crouched down and held out his little finger. "Pinkie promise." Bailey grinned with relief and climbed into Ben's father's truck.

"So I see you didn't think you could get them both into your car," observed McKenzie.

Ben shrugged. "I had to take a piece of furniture to the antique shop for Ms. Olivia today, plus—" he patted the hood of the old blue pickup "—Dad wanted to get a feel for a two-seater, now that he's thinking about retirement."

"Is he?" McKenzie lifted her brows.

"He's considering it," Ben admitted. "But it's a big decision. The clinic will have to close if he can't sell it to anyone."

"I'm sure somebody will step up," McKenzie declared. This wouldn't bode well for Bailey's emergencies, though.

"Yes, but until then, he'll be back to work part-time until after the recital."

The recital. The practice of the dance routine had been funny to watch, but McKenzie had forgotten what that meant. Christmas was around the corner. Soon, Ben would be gone. "Could you stay longer, considering your father's change of heart?"

"I can't." Ben's cheery expression faded. "I have to be back in Chicago the following Monday." The girls giggled from inside the truck.

"And Megan?"

"She knows. I promised to come back once a month." Ben looked around the parking lot as if he wanted to avoid eye contact. "I'll do it, too. Rack up some frequent-flyer miles."

"That'll be nice." McKenzie tried to smile,

but her chest turned to ice. She knew monthly visits were better than talking online on occasion, but in the depths of her heart, she'd hoped Ben would change his mind. For Megan's sake. That was what she wanted for Christmas, even more than a new job—Ben at home with his daughter. A silence fell between them, and she shivered. She wanted him to wrap his arms around her and warm her soul, but he didn't.

"I'm sorry there aren't any surgical units in Kudzu Creek," said Ben. She looked into his eyes and thought he meant it. "For Megan's sake, I mean."

"I'm sorry, too," McKenzie whispered but didn't say why.

Ben gave her a teasing nudge. "Maybe when I come back, there'll be a new bookstore."

McKenzie wagged her head at him. "No, but I hope I'll have something new and exciting to tell you about." She gave him a tremulous smile.

By Wednesday, Ben was relieved Bailey had an appointment so he could see McKenzie again. The girls' sleepover had gone wonderfully, and he had his mother to thank for it. McKenzie had picked up Bailey Saturday morning, and he'd forced himself to act like it was business as usual, but it was hard. Something had happened in the parking lot at the dance studio again. Something less than romantic. This time, he'd seen disappointment in McKenzie's eyes. She cared so much for his daughter that she was sorry to see him go. On Sunday, they'd sat together at church, then ate lunch together over at the Ainsworths'. Bradley had been excited about his company moving, and Donovan and Lindsey were happy to have him across the street from their inn. They all encouraged McKenzie on her job hunt, but the best opportunities seemed to be out of town, and Ben could tell that bothered her.

He could hardly sleep. Staying focused on his patients was a challenge. Between missing her when he shouldn't and the upcoming recital, where he'd have to perform in front of the town, anxiety was eating at him like a virus. Just venting to her would make him feel a little better.

"I guess I'll see you at the recital," he said as McKenzie tugged her purse up onto her shoulder after the appointment. Bailey skipped down the hall for her sticker from Darlene. Ben watched her go, then turned back to McKenzie.

She grinned. "You're going to do fine, Ben. Just focus on the back wall and smile. All of Kudzu Creek is looking forward to seeing young Dr. Cooper dance with his daughter."

"I think you mean my parents."

"No, I mean everyone else." Rather than laugh, McKenzie squeezed his arm. "You'll be great. Don't worry about the knuckleheads."

Ben snorted. "I won't. Especially since I've made peace with Scotty Dougherty. He even thanked me."

"Scotty thanked you?" McKenzie repeated. "You told me about the handshake, but he actually expressed gratitude?"

"He did, and I have you to thank for that."

"What do you mean?"

"You encouraged me when patients started canceling appointments because my dad couldn't see them."

"I'm proud of you for everything you've done. You should know that." McKenzie's eyes shimmered, and it made him glow inside.

"Maybe that's all I ever wanted—to make you proud," Ben whispered, yearning to kiss her again, right there in the middle of the clinic. But she dropped her gaze to the floor.

"Ben, I've never told you before, but I think you did the right thing leaving town. It's what you wanted and worked for, and I had no right to discourage you."

"You never discouraged me," he insisted.

"Aunt McKenzie, I'm ready to go," called Bailey.

Ben jumped at the interruption, wishing there was more time. Perhaps another day, he and McKenzie could go out to dinner. He just wouldn't call it a date. They could hang out. He opened his mouth to ask, but she stepped away, breaking the spell.

"I guess I'll see you later, then, Dr. Cooper." She waved goodbye and headed down the hall to join her niece. Ben watched her go. He was suddenly weighed down with remorse. If he had never left Kudzu Creek, things could have been different. He probably wouldn't have become a doctor, but he might have had a chance with the girl he'd loved then, and who he still loved now. She could have felt more than friendship for him over time—time that she'd needed. He suddenly blamed himself for always being in such a rush. With a sigh, Ben stumbled toward his office, only to find the light blinking on his father's antiquated answering machine. "There's a call for you from Ohio," Darlene called from down the hall. He furrowed his brow as his heart picked up its sagging pace. The only people he knew there were at Ohio State East Hospital.

Chapter Thirteen

Nine days before Christmas, the house lights of the high school auditorium dimmed, and McKenzie, Jill and Diane halted their discussion of Bailey's dance photos, which they'd just seen for the first time. "Oh, did I tell you," Claire whispered suddenly from a few seats down, "that Brad saw a bookstore in downtown Columbus that is looking for a store manager?"

McKenzie leaned over Diane. "Is it an indie store?"

"No, but they serve coffee and cookies. It's right across the street from the river."

McKenzie raised her brows. "I'll have to check it out. Thanks."

"It'd be perfect for you," Diane agreed. "You have a gift for keeping things running."

McKenzie smiled at the compliment just as music began to blast from the auditorium speakers. She clenched the armrest. It was not only her niece's first recital but Megan's, too. McKenzie's mouth stretched into a smile with the anticipation of Ben's dance number. He no longer seemed to have the chip on his shoulder he'd carried into town. He'd definitely come a long way, from the boy who avoided attention at all costs to a man who would dance with his daughter just to entertain his friends. It was as if he'd made peace with the ghosts of yesterday. He'd even taken to driving his father's truck around town and downsized from an all-slacks wardrobe to the occasional blue jeans, which made him even more attractive.

Other women had begun to notice him, too, and not just her friends in the Kudzu Creek Book Club. McKenzie had watched heads turn when he walked into the final practice in the old high school auditorium that afternoon. His hair gleamed like sandalwood, his lightly freckled skin was tanned from weekend runs, and his arms were slender but muscular from helping out on the family farm. Her heart lurched, and she wondered if it was the anticipation of watching him dance with Megan or seeing him brave a dance onstage in front of the whole town—the very same stage where he'd once invited her to share his life. She looked down the row of seats. On the other side of Diane,

Ms. Olivia held her cane, and Claire and Lindsey were finishing up a whispered conversation. They weren't just there for the children, she knew. They wanted to support the nervous young Dr. Cooper as well.

Her throat tightened. He did belong in a hospital. His kindness and compassion did so much for others struggling or in pain—just like he'd done for her, a little girl wandering through life practically alone. And he'd let her into his circle of trust, listening and laughing and confiding and challenging her. What a blessing he'd been in her childhood. Her teen years. Young adulthood. What a fool she'd been to let him go. At the very least, she should have considered her feelings for him and Athens before shutting him down cold.

Regret crept like bile up into her mouth as the first darlings pranced their way through the opening number. McKenzie tried to concentrate on the dance routines, but her pulse skipped anxiously while she waited to see Ben on stage. Her Ben. She'd been wrong to misjudge him, to make assumptions. Career training, a broken marriage and raising a child were enormous things to juggle, even one at a time. She scanned the audience, seeing mothers and fathers, men and women, friends and lovers, and her stomach clanked into the bottom of her soul as it echoed with emptiness.

Finally, the children pranced out in their tap shoes and costumes for the next act. A line of fathers followed them from behind, and the audience broke into peals of laughter. McKenzie smiled. There he was. Front and center. Red-faced Ben Cooper, all grown up. The music began and filled her heart as Ben danced with his daughter rather awkwardly, flushing and vulnerable and brave for all the world to see. Megan was beaming like a Christmas tree star. McKenzie's cheeks went hot, and her eyes blurred. Jill elbowed her in the darkness of the auditorium as the audience jumped to their feet in explosive applause at the final dance pose. "Are you okay?

McKenzie watched Ben take his bows with the rest of the dance team. His face was so red even his ears glowed. A tear escaped with a giggle. She loved him. "I'm—I'm not sure," McKenzie stammered, her soul on fire and her mind pulling in a hundred different directions. "But I know that's the best dance number I've ever seen."

Ben found Megan at Bailey's side just as he expected when he made his way out into the auditorium after the program. Her face was still sparkling with glittery makeup that made her look more comical than adult. His parents were in deep conversation with McKenzie and Jill. "Well," he said, bracing himself, "what'd you think?"

His mother broke into applause, but Dad threw his head back and laughed before patting his son on the back. "Let's just say you better stick to doctoring," he guffawed with tears of amusement in his eyes.

From the middle of the row of seats, Ms. Olivia waved her cane in the air to get Ben's attention. "That was the best dance number I've seen since Laurel Murphy's husband lip-synced with a boy band for the addiction-recovery's spring benefit." Diane hooted in laughter.

Ben reminded himself it was all in good fun and grinned at McKenzie's examining stare. "I've never been so humiliated in all my life," he admitted.

"You came through it with flying colors," she promised. "It wasn't half-bad." Her gaze sank into his, then flitted toward his parents as if there was more she wanted to say.

"We were going to go to dinner," said Ben, hoping she would agree to come. "Would you like to join us?" He looked down the row at the other ladies. "Everyone's invited."

"We'd love to," said Jill, a little too fast. She

glanced at McKenzie, who seemed to flush under the house lights.

"Sure," agreed McKenzie in a casual tone. "I think Bailey and Megan would like that."

"How about Southern Fried Kudzu," suggested Dad. "They've just announced they're staying open later."

Ben watched the expression on McKenzie's face frost over. "No," he said quickly.

She waved him off. "It's okay."

"Oh, I'm sorry, we forgot," gasped Ben's mother. She gave Ben's father a sideways look of reproach. "It's so hard to remember you're not there anymore."

"No. It's fine," said McKenzie. "I think I'm ready now. Bradley Ainsworth was in Columbus recently and saw an indie bookstore there that needed a manager. I have other options on the table."

"Yes, I just told her about it," interjected Claire.

"That's great news," said Ben's mom. Ben felt his cheek tug with a smile. McKenzie was considering leaving Kudzu Creek? He was proud of her. It'd be a big change. And he had one ahead of him now, too. He just hoped they all would understand.

Everyone retired to their cars and drove from the high school to downtown, parking side by side in front of the diner, which, to Ben's surprise, was not bustling as usual. That was best, he decided, as there would be less of a wait, and they could all talk. He hoped his big announcement wouldn't outshine the performances of his daughter and her best friend.

With canned Christmas music echoing overhead, the group ordered at the counter in a small mob with an employee who looked rather frazzled and, thankfully, didn't seem to recognize McKenzie. Bailey added to the chaos with a sudden cry. "I forgot my duffel bag!"

McKenzie shushed her. "Don't worry, we'll go back and get it." She waved at Barney in the pass-through window.

Ben thought he looked tired and disgruntled. "I wonder what Barney's doing here, working so late," he said in a low tone as they gathered around a large table at the front window. They scooted in chairs to fit.

"Maybe someone else took the morning shift," McKenzie suggested.

Jill walked over after calming Bailey down, and Ben watched the sisters ease into their seats shoulder to shoulder. Megan and Bailey left a vacancy on McKenzie's other side as if Ben sitting next to her was expected. Nervously, he sat down.

"Barney has started up the grill since before I was around." McKenzie absentmindedly looked about the room. Ben watched her study tables still stacked with empty dishes and dirty napkins. The trash receptacle in the corner was heaped full and about to spill over. Her jaw seemed to grow tighter and tighter.

"Don't do it," murmured Ben.

She looked sideways. "Do what?"

"You're about to get up and start cleaning."

She exhaled. "Look at it. This isn't the place I remember."

"You mean the place you grew up in or the same place as last month?"

"Both, I guess." She frowned and turned her attention back to the conversation as Ben did his best to distract her, but she was tense. Even though he loved the feeling of Megan sitting so close, he wanted to snake his free arm around McKenzie's waist and pull her to him on the other side. To have both girls in either arm would be a heady feeling. Ben's chest pinched. *Impossible.* Megan giggled and whispered in Bailey's ear. Everyone was sipping their drinks while waiting for their order numbers to be called, and Ben decided it was time. He interrupted them by clearing his throat. "I have an announcement."

His parents looked at him in surprise, and McKenzie straightened with curiosity. Ben reached for Megan like she was a safety line and pulled her onto his lap. His little girl didn't resist. She rested her head back against his chest, and he could feel her tiny heartbeat thumping with contentment under his embrace. He would not let go. Leaving McKenzie behind was hard enough.

"I got a fellowship offer."

Everyone gasped. Dad said, "Well, congratulations. Was it better than my offer?"

McKenzie stared. "Your dad offered you a job?"

Ben winced but tried to make it look like a smile. "Yes, the clinic, so he doesn't have to sell it to a stranger." He looked apologetically at his parents. "But it's not a surgery center, unfortunately."

Across the table, Jill clasped her fingers together and rested her chin on her fist. "I hope it's in Atlanta or nearby." Ben didn't miss her glance at her sister beside her. McKenzie seemed to be holding her breath, along with the rest of the table.

"Well, tell us, then!" blustered Ms. Olivia.

"Ohio State East called."

His mom gasped and covered her mouth. "That was your first choice!" she said between her fingers. Ben felt his face split into a happy grin.

"Well, outside of Chicago. They have a position, and I've been offered it if I can get up there by the first of the year."

His mother jumped up and circled the table to wrap her arms around him in a crushing hug. "I'm so proud of you," she choked. Dad's eyes shone. Ben looked at McKenzie, unable to keep from beaming, but deep down, his gut trembled. She was not smiling. She sat rigidly and blinked, looking anywhere but at him.

"Congratulations, Ben," she stammered. Her tone sounded empty, her mood deflated. Ben recoiled. He knew she thought he should stay for Megan, but she was happy about his progress with his daughter. She was proud of him—she'd said so. A burst of static crackled overhead, and he jumped. The young woman at the counter announced his parents' order number, and Ben's Dad scooted out of his chair to retrieve the food with a nod at McKenzie. "You were right. The new intercom system *is* inconvenient."

She gave a swift nod but kept her gaze on the table. After all the arguments they'd had, and all their resolutions, Ben knew she was confused as to why he still wanted to go. It must have hurt a little, he guessed, even if she was not in love with him, that he still had plans that did not include her or Kudzu Creek. But he was doing the right thing. Wasn't he? His chest knotted. "That's not all," he said carefully. He looked back at his mother and braced himself, clutching Megan for support. "I'm going to take Megan with me."

"What?" His mom gasped in surprise.

"Take her where?" demanded Bailey.

"Shh!" said Jill.

McKenzie straightened beside him. "You can't take Megan to Ohio. She has dance class, her friends at school and Bailey."

"And Jiminy," exclaimed Bailey.

Megan bent back her head to peer up at him. "I don't want to go, Daddy. What about Grandma?"

"Grandma will be just fine, and we'll visit a lot from our new house. Okay?"

Mom's eyes misted over, and without warning, Bailey stood up beside her chair and began to wail. Another number was announced over the speakers as his father walked up with a teetering tray and said, "What happened?" McKenzie jumped up and stalked out without reply, pushing the front door open and bolting down the sidewalk.

"Oh no," murmured Diane.

Ms. Olivia rapped the table with her cane, a loud, cracking sound that quieted the room. She glared at Ben. "And what am *I* supposed to do?"

"Oh my, w-we should—" stammered Jill in

the shocked silence. She reached for Bailey. "We should get our food to go." Bailey began to cry louder. Megan began to whimper.

"But, Daddy, Kudzu Creek is our home. I don't want to go." His daughter twisted around in his arms to look out the door, where McKenzie had disappeared. "Where did McKenzie go?" She put her hands over her face and began to cry. "Where's Mac? I don't want to leave her."

And for the first time since he'd been helping people in crisis, Ben didn't know what to do.

McKenzie hurried to the car and jumped inside. She could think of nothing but driving as far away and as fast as she could, but that wasn't possible. Her life was here. She dropped her head on the steering wheel as she turned the key in the ignition, cringing from the pain in her throat that was holding back a deluge. With a loud sob, she exhaled and took a rattling breath as she backed out of the parking spot to head home. Before she'd gone a block, though, she remembered she'd promised to return to the high school to pick up Bailey's duffel. She pulled over. Tears gushed, but she let them stream, swiping at her eyes so she could see down the highway after turning around. Ben was leaving. Again. And this time, she didn't want him to go without her. She loved him. He made her happy, eased her chaos, made her feel safe and brave and…finished. Like a piece of art. A five-star meal. A symphony. A dance. They were a good team. And from the way he'd made her feel when he kissed her, she knew they could be an incredibly happy couple if she made the move.

Pain clutched her chest with dull, stabbing fingers as her old car whirred into the night. Part of her wanted to drive out to the creek and hide there. Any lingering hope that Ben would change his mind about leaving was dashed—and worse, her heart was crushed because he hadn't asked her to go with him this time. But why would he? He wasn't in love with her anymore. That was a lifetime ago. A memory. Instead, he was taking his little girl, whom she happened to love, too. So actually, she was losing both Megan and her father. A piece of her heart and a chunk of her soul. It was all messed up. All wrong.

Another sob escaped. McKenzie shivered and realized she'd left her jacket at the diner. Rather than dial up the heat, she let her sadness warm her until she pulled into the back of the old auditorium. She slammed the car door after she climbed out and wiped her face with her arm. She needed to be strong. Resolute.

The back entrance was locked, so she walked around the building while trembling in the cold. As she reached for the door to the lobby, she glanced up at the night sky. It was muddled and dark. Clouds were gathering, and there wasn't a star in sight. The hope of a joyous Christmas had dimmed. *Perfectly dismal,* she thought. She gave a small hiccup and let herself in. A few stragglers were still wandering the halls or talking in groups. McKenzie made a beeline for the auditorium. One of the school janitors was polishing the floors in the foyer, but he didn't complain when she pulled open the door to let herself in. He was probably ready to go home to his family.

The giant auditorium was empty. She walked down the aisle to the row where they'd sat but didn't see a duffel bag. Turning to the heavy curtains, she spotted the bag sitting on the stage, as if someone had found it and knew its owner would come looking for it. She grabbed the bag and walked back to the front row, collapsed in the first seat and then dropped her head back. There weren't any stars offering hope on the ceiling, either. McKenzie closed her eyes, and another tear streamed down her cheek in a soggy rivulet. She'd lost the job she'd wanted to turn into a career, and the man she'd fallen in love with was no longer in love with her. She swallowed painfully, her mind as thick as mud. She would miss the diner, but it was Ben—who was not only leaving but also taking Megan with him—she would mourn the rest of her life.

It felt like desertion. Like her mother leaving, a person who loved her deep down but needed to go. Like her father's cold indifference, fueled by a need for more and more and more. Jill had found Tim. McKenzie had found nothing and no one.

For the first time in her life, McKenzie knew she was not okay. She'd forced herself to be independent. Strong. Willing to sacrifice everything to make everyone else happy. But she wanted someone who would give, too, and no one would do but Ben.

McKenzie slowly opened her eyes at a scuffling sound coming down the aisle. Sheepishly, she wiped her cheeks and tried to think of an excuse for the poor janitor. Her heart hitched in her chest when she saw it was Ben. He had his hands in his pockets, his face was taut and his eyes were wide with concern. He backed a few steps away to rest against a chair in the next section. "Are you okay, Mac?"

His tender tone made it hurt more. McKenzie redirected her attention to the darkened stage, where only minutes before, fathers and daughters had been smiling and dancing. "Yes, I'm fine. It just came as a shock."

"I know you care about Megan. That's one of the things I love most about you." Ben eased his hands out of his pockets. "You know I was only here temporarily."

"To help your father—yes, I know." She looked at him, trying to hide her pain. "He offered you the clinic?"

"He wants to retire now. It's decided."

McKenzie returned her gaze to the stage—the place where she and Ben had made beautiful music together in their youth. "It was never enough for you, Kudzu Creek." She gave him a pained stare. "We were never enough."

He frowned. "McKenzie, you were always enough for me. I'm sorry I need more. I have more to do."

She furrowed her brow. "More what? People need surgery in this county, too, you know. There's a hospital in Albany."

Ben shuffled his feet and stared at the floor. "I have other reasons for going, McKenzie. Reasons you don't want to hear."

"What's that supposed to mean?"

"It means if my fellowship offer is in Ohio and I can take my daughter with me, it's best that I go."

"But Megan, too?" More tears welled up.

McKenzie let them go, wishing she could plead with Ben to stay, but there was no use. The only woman he wanted in his life right now was his little girl, and she couldn't blame him for that. It was as it should be. It was what she'd wanted for Megan from the beginning.

Ben hoisted himself up and walked over to slip down into the chair on the other side of her. When he reached for her hand, McKenzie laced her fingers through his, and they stared into the darkness. Suddenly, she saw the stage as he must have that day in high school: blinding lights and hundreds of faces staring at him while he grasped for the courage to ask a girl for more than friendship. She would have never had the nerve. "You're very, very brave," she said at last. "I wish I could be more like you."

"That job in the Columbus bookstore Claire mentioned?" he said quietly. "You're a great supervisor, McKenzie, and you'd do awesome managing a bookstore."

She shook her head, which was filled with doubt. "Maybe, but it's so far, and that would affect Jill and Bailey's lives. Plus, I'd see them so much less." She sighed. "I'd probably end up having to move there."

"And you'd find mysteries, romances and adventures all within the safe bindings of their book covers. Your family will be all right. It's not that far."

McKenzie shut her eyes and indulged in her imagination. "It would be a job I'd love," she admitted, "even if the business wasn't mine."

"Yet." Ben was ever the optimist. If he'd taught her anything, it was to believe in possibilities, no matter the forecasted outlook.

"I suppose you're right."

"And they have diners," Ben teased. He squeezed her fingers.

"Right, more diners." She exhaled slowly, loving the feeling of his palm against hers. "But nothing like Southern Fried Kudzu with Barney at the grill."

He turned to study her, and she met his stare. His cheek curled into a smile. "Maybe Barney would come along."

She choked out a laugh. "Just promise us you'll bring Megan back as often as possible."

He shook her hand a little, raised it as if he meant to bring it to his lips, then set it back down. Her heart deflated even further. "I promise," he whispered.

Chapter Fourteen

Ben left for the final interview and to fill out paperwork for his new position over the weekend, leaving Megan behind. She'd promised to finish reading the rest of *Chicken Little* to Jiminy. She was becoming proficient with her sight words, and he decided to make sure they had a good bookstore in their new hometown. After the interview and paperwork, he drove by a few renovated, shotgun-style homes, but nothing looked appropriate for a six-year-old who loved animals and dancing.

The loud traffic around the hospital was different from Kudzu Creek, and he had to remind himself to be patient as he tapped the steering wheel of the rental car. The closest dance studio was a drive, but it was nice. There was a bookstore just two doors down. By the time he flew back to Atlanta and pulled into his parents' driveway Monday afternoon, the sun was setting behind the pastures, making the house glow tangerine around the edges. The family Christmas tree glowed through the window, and the strings of lights he'd framed around the windows and porch blinked peacefully in the silent dusk. He was surprised how good it felt to be home even though he'd landed the distinguished fellowship in Ohio. Maybe it was because he knew Mom would have dinner simmering in the kitchen. Dad would be watching his favorite game show, shouting out wrong answers, and his daughter...

She came out the door as if his heart had bidden her. Megan held a book in her hand, looking much like McKenzie as a little girl. Her dark hair was in a ponytail, and with a small smile, he noted she wore a pair of mismatched socks. They were from the same mold—that much was true. Even if they didn't share the same blood. Megan turned and gazed up at the blinking lights with wonder, then set the book on the front porch swing. To his surprise, she threw her arms up over her head and began to twirl around the porch. Ben recognized the dance routine they'd danced together. She reached her hand out for an imaginary partner who wasn't there. His throat knotted. *But, Daddy, Kudzu Creek is our home.* Ben sucked in a breath and let himself out of the sports car, which suddenly felt like a prison.

The late afternoon was quiet, with no noise other than circling crows in the distance, the faint mumbles of the animals in the backyard and a slight creaking from the front porch swing as it rocked on its chains. Then he heard it: the faint chorus of "O Little Town of Bethlehem" echoing from the radio in the living room. *The hopes and fears of all the years…* He swept his gaze from Megan to the flat fields and tree line in the distance. Everything in Kudzu Creek seemed to grow right, even coming full circle if it stumbled off track. *Including Scotty Dougherty*, he thought. Ben watched his daughter dance alone. Would a professional dance instructor and private school bring her more happiness than a life in this town? Suddenly, Ben saw his father as a young man, fresh out of medical school, with options laid out before him like a career buffet, and he had chosen Kudzu Creek. He could have gone farther and done so much more. But in whose eyes? Being a country doctor was what his father had wanted. Ben even thought it was a good idea until… His chest felt heavy. He couldn't take

Megan away from this, but he could not bear the thought of letting her go, either. *What do I want more? What matters most?*

He realized Megan was watching him, and their gazes locked. "Daddy!" Megan shouted. He loved her so much. He strode across the yard and hopped up onto the porch, arms outstretched.

He crouched, and she ran straight to him. After she threw herself into his arms, she clutched him tightly, and Ben let his wet eyes seep out from the corners. Taking an excited breath, Megan reared back and looked him in the eye. "I'm so glad you're home."

Ben picked her up and held her under the twinkling lights. "I'm glad to be home, too—but most of all, I'm happy to see you." He danced silently with her for a moment, listening to a new Christmas song echoing from his home.

"I thought you went with Grandpa."

"I was in Ohio, remember?"

"Yes, but he told Grandma to tell you to come."

"To come where?" asked Ben with concern.

"To the doctor's office where Bailey goes."

Ben peered into her eyes. "What happened at the clinic, Megan?"

"Ms. Olive is sick."

"Ms. Olivia?" Ben clarified.

She nodded. "Are they going to call an ambulance?"

"I don't know," Ben responded, setting her down. His mother came out on the porch, wiping her hands on a wet dish towel. "What's going on?"

Mom gave her head a small shake. "Ms. Olivia fell, Ben. And she refuses to leave town and go to a hospital unless you ride with her."

Ben let a small groan escape. "No one called me."

"Your phone is going straight to voice mail."

Ben tried to recall if he'd turned his phone back on after his flight had landed. He'd been in an enormous hurry to get his luggage and race home to see his daughter and tell her about the dance studio he'd found. "You go on inside with Grandma, Megan," he told her. He looked up at his mother. "Call Dad and tell him I'm on my way over."

By the time he rolled into Kudzu Creek, dusk had settled and there was a small crowd in front of the clinic. A silent ambulance was parked outside, its spinning lights illuminating the night. He zoomed into the nearest parking spot, jumped out and rushed for the front door. Nearby, Diane and Vi, had linked arms and were whispering to one another, faces strobing in the emergency lights. Before he could ask questions, the clinic door opened, and Claire and McKenzie rushed out.

Seeing McKenzie whooshed the air from Ben's lungs. She looked as white as a ghost as the lights flashed on her face, but then she saw him and relief flooded her features. She raced over. "I'm so glad you're here," she cried, clutching his arms. Seeing her made Ben's chest feel like it was going to explode. He'd only been gone a weekend, yet here she was, making him feel like she was the oxygen he needed to survive.

He struggled to focus. "Is she okay? What happened?"

"I found her." Claire took his elbow and pulled Ben toward the door. "I didn't see Ms. Olivia this morning on her usual walk, and around dinnertime, I noticed I hadn't seen her on the porch, having tea. My neighbor next door, Mr. Thu, heard her dog barking for what seemed like forever so he went over and knocked. When she didn't answer, he came and got me because I have a key."

"Did you find her conscious?"

"Yes, she'd slipped in the kitchen and fallen on her hip. I think it's—well, she's in a great deal of pain, but your father and the paramedics were able to transport her here after she refused to go to the hospital." Ben glanced toward the waiting ambulance. "Your father promised her you were on the way," Claire continued, "so she agreed to let them call a unit to take her to Albany once you arrived."

"Where's her son?" Ben struggled to remember the name of Ms. Olivia's only child, whom she'd explained lived in the next county over.

"He's out of town but catching the next flight."

"If it's bad, she'll end up in Atlanta, won't she?" interjected McKenzie with apprehension.

Ben stared into her eyes. They shone as navy blue as the ocean at night. Worry hovered around her in a halo he could almost see. "Don't worry about Ms. Olivia," he said, trying to console her. "I'll do everything I can."

Ben slipped inside, fighting the urge he felt to take McKenzie in his arms, kiss her forehead and tell her everything would be okay. He took a deep breath and strode through the dimly lit lobby to the back hall. The light was on in room number one. A paramedic came out with wide eyes and flushed cheeks. "How is she?" Ben demanded.

"As full of spit and vinegar as ever," the

young man groaned. Ben smiled. Clearly, the medics had tried to sell Ms. Olivia something she didn't want to buy. He rounded the corner, hoping things weren't as bad as they seemed, and found his father leaning over a gurney, peering into the frail, white face of a woman wrapped like a mummy in warming blankets. There was a backboard under her body, and her waist was secured with stabilizing sheets. "Dad!" Ben grabbed his father's attention, and his father straightened, putting a hand on his side as if his ribs pained him. "What happened?"

Ben listened carefully as Dad explained, seeing in his mind's eye exactly what had transpired with his favorite patient that he'd somehow inherited. "I thought the new meds I prescribed her would steady her," he said in a low tone. The accident made him feel responsible and guilty.

"Dr. Cooper? Is that my new doctor?" screeched a strained voice. "It wasn't my meds, it was Snoopy. I tripped over that uppity old tomcat!"

Ben moved closer to the bed and peered into Ms. Olivia's face. "How are you, Olivia?" he asked in a soothing tone.

From out of the folds of the blanket, Mrs.

Olivia retorted, "That's Ms. Olivia, Ben Cooper—now don't you go getting all familiar!"

Dad laughed, and Ben's face heated. "I'm sorry, ma'am," he said quickly. "I was so worried I forgot who I was talking to."

"How can you forget me? I called for you, didn't I?"

"Yes, and here I am, all the way back from Ohio. Now, would you tell me exactly what happened? In your own words."

"Ohio?" complained Ms. Olivia instead. "What were you doing there? Isn't your little girl here?"

"Yes, she is, but—"

"And your momma and daddy?"

"Yes, but—"

"Oh, Ben Cooper," scolded Ms. Olivia; then she gasped and sucked in a breath, crinkling in pain. "So is McKenzie!" It came out in a quiet wheeze, and Ben pretended not to hear it. He reached for Ms. Olivia's hand and held it.

"We need to get you to the hospital, Ms. Olivia," he insisted. "Then we'll decide what to do next."

"I'm not going to Atlanta," she cried in an uncharacteristic manner, and her pale eyes glistened as they filled with tears. She squeezed his hand. "Don't let them take me to the big city,

Dr. Cooper. They'll forget about me there. I'll end up in some home for broken folks far away from Kudzu Creek."

"We won't forget about you, and you'll get good treatment there."

"Let's just go to Albany," Dad suggested.

"It's the closest," agreed Ben.

"Well," said Ms. Oliva, shutting her eyes as her voice grew faint, "Albany wouldn't be so bad if you come. But first, take me somewhere where I can lie down in a real bed. Please?"

"We can do that in Albany," said Ben. "In the emergency room. And the X-rays will be a breeze. They'll give you medicine, and you won't feel a thing."

Ms. Olivia jerked her eyes open. "I want to feel, Dr. Cooper. If I don't hurt, I won't know whether I'm alive or not."

Ben backed away as the words sank in. "I'll let the paramedics know," he said to his father, "and we'll get her wheeled out." Ben reached for his phone, scrolling through his lists of contacts who might know someone in the Albany area. He wanted to find the best treatment for Ms. Olivia, whom he knew only wanted what was best for him. *If I don't hurt, I won't know whether I'm alive or not.* He could relate. He'd made it a point in medical school not to feel too much. In a way, he'd made himself numb in Chicago, too. For years. He hadn't felt anything in Ohio this past weekend, either. He only felt alive when he was home in Kudzu Creek. Even when it hurt. His mind whirled over his patient and daughter and the woman he was falling for all over again. It was an impossible dilemma. What was a father and doctor and best friend to do?

Two days later, while Jill was at work and Bailey was in school, McKenzie drove into town and parked in front of Alabaster's. After Ms. Olivia's accident, she'd decided not to call the bookstore in Columbus. Diane had offered her work, and it meant she could stay close to home for now. She would be ready to help Ms. Olivia when she returned and could worry about a job later. McKenzie hadn't told Ben. She hadn't heard from him and didn't want to bother him. He'd quit texting her after they'd parted ways outside the high school auditorium, and he hadn't kept her informed about Ms. Olivia. Part of her felt like what they had rekindled was beginning to wither—a hope that had bloomed since late fall was dying in the bottom of her heart. At least she could admit it now.

She walked to Alabaster's, feeling heavy and cold, and she wrapped her sweater around herself as she reached for the handle to the shop's front door. She frowned as she noticed there was no lunch line trickling out of Southern Fried Kudzu. No one stood at the register inside Diane's shop, either, so she perused ceramics shelves displaying Claire's pottery pieces that looked like they belonged in a museum. McKenzie picked up a salsa bowl and admired it. Art was Claire's passion, and together, she and Bradley made it work. Just like Ben had made his career path work. And everyone else around her. Alabaster's was Diane's dream. *What am I so afraid of?* she wondered.

"Oh, there you are. I thought I heard the front door." Diane darted in from the back of the store and scooted through the aisle between display tables to meet McKenzie. "What do you think about Claire's work? Isn't it gorgeous?"

"It is. She's so passionate."

"That's why she's in a good mood all the time," observed Diane. "She has an outlet." She looped her arm through McKenzie's and guided her toward the stools behind the register. "Come sit with me. I want to talk."

"About the holiday schedule, I presume?" guessed McKenzie. "I can put in four hours today until Bailey and Megan get out."

"Because you're not in Columbus."

"I've decided not to apply," said McKenzie.

"Oh, good." Diane's remark caught her by surprise.

"What do you mean?"

"I mean after I thought about it, I can't imagine you being happy driving an hour that way and back—not with all you do for Bailey and how much time you spend with Jill."

"Exactly," breathed McKenzie. "You understand me. I just don't want to live far away from them. From here. Not alone."

Diane picked up a pen and flipped it around in her fingers. "That's what I admire about you, McKenzie. You know your own heart and stay true to it. Not many do."

McKenzie sighed. "I'm not sure if you're right."

Diane was quiet for a moment. "I called Jill," she admitted, "after last weekend to see if you were all right."

McKenzie looked up. "She didn't mention it."

"Everyone in the book club wanted to call when you ran out of the diner after the dance recital, but I told them to give you some breathing room. It was clear you were upset about Ben taking Megan away. We missed you at church, too."

"Yes," said McKenzie, her cheeks warming so much she couldn't meet Diane's eyes.

"I just wondered—I mean, I don't want to pry because I know you're very private, but I wondered if you were also upset that Ben is leaving again, too."

"I knew he would be," said McKenzie.

"Did you think he would change his mind?"

McKenzie fought the urge to wilt at her question. "I suppose a part of me hoped he would, especially after…" She couldn't bring herself to admit she'd kissed him when they weren't even in a relationship. "He left once before," she explained, now flushing all over, "and I let him go."

"I thought it was something like that."

"I practically sent him on his way, but this time, I—" McKenzie's eyes watered. "I'm sorry, but I just don't want him to go. It's devastating to me."

"Have you told him?"

"Told him what?"

"That you love him."

McKenzie's cheeks caught fire, and the heat traveled down her neck. It was true. She couldn't deny it anymore. "In a way."

Diane stared back with wide eyes, waiting for more. McKenzie blurted out, "Okay, I only told him I wished he would stay. I didn't tell him that since he's been home, I've fallen completely in love with him and see no way out."

"He probably felt the same way once."

"He had it rough in school. Other kids gave him a hard time because he was smart, studious and, of course, because his father was a doctor. They lived more comfortably than a lot of his patients, you see."

"People grow up."

"Yes, and they have." McKenzie thought of the Doughertys.

"Growing up is hard for anyone, no matter what the circumstances are. There's no reason for him not to feel welcome here now."

"I suppose not. I mean, I think he does."

"But does he have a reason to stay?" Diane pressed.

"There's Megan." McKenzie began to feel like her excuses were a defense. "But he's taking her with him now."

Diane looked at her with mild exasperation. "He's taking Megan with him because he can. She'll be all right, but will you?"

"I don't know."

After a pause, Diane said, "Okay. Well, then, I know you aren't a big gambler, but I have something I want to show you."

"What's that?"

Diane dug into the register and pulled out a key ring and waved it in the air. "Come with me." She slipped off her stool and led the way out the door. They walked next door to the construction company office. It was dark inside. The lettering of the company had been peeled off the windows.

"What are we doing?"

"I asked the realtor for the key. I thought we could take a look inside."

"You've decided to expand Alabaster's after all."

Diane gave her a mysterious smile. "Not exactly, but it's a space I wanted you to see."

Chapter Fifteen

Ben left the hospital in Albany again with a mix of satisfaction. Ms. Olivia was receiving the treatment she needed, although he was worried about her being so far from home. But he knew this was the best place for her. Her son and the local church congregation had already worked out a visitation schedule. Even her book club friends made daily phone calls. Today the wise woman had patted his hand while he tried to comfort her, only asking that he not forget about her. She would have to spend some time in physical therapy before she returned to Kudzu Creek. There was a tough road ahead. It made Ben sad he wouldn't be able to stay and follow her treatment, but not as sad as he'd felt seeing McKenzie outside the clinic with her face creased with concern. He wouldn't be seeing her anymore, either.

When he got home, Ben found Megan in the backyard, and he wandered across the dormant lawn, anxious to ask her about her day. "Megan!" he called out. His daughter waved and returned to a private conversation with her donkey. When he reached her, he leaned over the fence and ran his fingers through the animal's mane. "How's Jiminy today?"

"He's hungry." She offered the mangy animal another carrot and crooned when he stuck his big buck teeth out and bit into it. "Daddy," she asked, "can we take Jiminy with us? He doesn't like Grandpa, and Grandma is scared of him."

Ben laughed and crouched to her level. "Well, there won't be anywhere to keep him. We'll live in a big city, but there are pigeons that come and go."

"That's nice," she said, "but we have pigeons at the park."

"Yes, that's true." Ben opened his mouth to tell her about the new dance studio he'd found for her, but she cut him off.

"Daddy, I don't want to go to Ohio. Please. You can live here and still be a doctor." She looked at him with serious, desperate eyes, brown bangs fluttering across her square forehead. He realized the ends of her hair brushed the top of her sweater now. Her thick hair was growing. And so was she. Did childhood ever take a moment to stand still?

"I suppose I could," he allowed.

"Kudzu Creek is home. Jiminy needs us."

"So does Ms. Olivia," Ben admitted. He winked at her. "Did you know she wouldn't talk to any doctor but me? She says I'm the best doctor she ever had."

"You're the best doctor I know," said Megan loyally. She wagged her head. "I told my teacher you're a doctor, and she said you helped her sister get better. And Bailey said that you're her favorite doctor, too."

Ben smiled. "That was nice of her." Honest pride flooded over him. It mattered. It really did.

"Plus, Miss McKenzie said that you're the best man she's ever known, and I'm the luckiest girl in the world to have a daddy like you."

"Miss McKenzie said that?"

Megan nodded. "That's why I let you come to my dance class."

Ben burst into a chuckle and put a hand over his mouth to cover it. "That was nice of her to say. I love Miss McKenzie," he confessed. The world came to a stop. Ben's chest flooded with warmth and relief. It was cleansing to say it out loud. His feelings for her had never died, and now they were as strong as ever. He bit his lip as flames flickered to life in his chest. He was in love with McKenzie Price. *Again*.

"Why don't you marry her?" His daughter gave him a teasing grin and giggled. "That's what we say at school if you say you love something."

Ben pretended to laugh with her, hoping she couldn't detect how sheepish she'd made him feel. "Maybe you're right, Megan," he said, and when her mouth dropped open, he pointed at her. "I *mean* about staying home. Maybe I should stay in Kudzu Creek. I could buy a house here, work at the clinic for Ms. Olivia—" he joked "—and help you take care of Jiminy."

She studied him with concern written across her face. "Would my mommy live here?"

The innocent question thumped Ben back to reality. "Not that mommy," he said, trying to hide his sadness, "but maybe a new mommy someday," he promised her. It was a promise to himself, too. It was time to move on, to let himself love again. Not just for Megan's sake but for his own. Ben looked out across the field where he'd played as a boy and pressed his lips together to keep from chewing on the inside of his cheek. He was home, and come what may, he would stay. McKenzie had been right. There were surgeries in this part of the world, too. Whether he found love with her or they remained friends, he could not leave this place again. Not now, anyway. Not this month. His heart stilled, and for the first time in many years, he felt a peace only Christmas could bring.

Ben's father stepped into the office, pulling a stethoscope from his neck. It was his first half-day back, and he'd have the holiday weekend to rest. "Are you sure about this?"

"Are you?" Ben deadpanned. His earlier peace had not left him, but his stomach felt knotted over the monumental decision he'd just made. His Christmas dilemma was behind him. He would not be taking Megan with him; he would be staying in Kudzu Creek. And of course, that meant he would share his hometown with McKenzie once again.

"There's no one I trust to sell my clinic to more than my own son."

"It just goes against everything I thought I wanted." Ben smiled. "And to turn down a fellowship?" He sighed. "Like I said last night, I know you would find someone else eventually to take over the clinic, but Megan is happy here. Taking her away from you and Mom isn't fair, and me not being here for her isn't right, either. She would be miserable without her animals, even with an opportunity to take lessons in a professional dance studio."

"But will *you* be happy?" Dad looked hesitant. "I'm happy, but I want you to be satisfied, too."

Ben nodded slowly. "Yes. I will be. I was in such a rush to leave this town I forgot that there were parts of it that I loved, parts that made me who I am, and that made me a better person."

"You mean like McKenzie?" His father studied him knowingly.

Ben winced but allowed a small nod of acceptance. "She doesn't want me to leave. We were friends for so long, and to be friends again—to clear the air—is something special I don't think either one of us want to give up."

"But you still love her."

Ben smiled weakly. He would wait as long as he could for McKenzie's feelings to change, but he wouldn't pressure her with his own again. "Unfortunately. But I'll get over it, eventually." His father chuckled but pretended it was a cough. "I'd rather have her in my life as a friend than not have her in my life at all. I'll learn to live with it," Ben insisted. "I have to—for Megan's sake. And the hospital in Albany isn't that far if I decide to return to the operating tables."

His father harrumphed. Ben didn't want

to talk about it anymore, so he let it go. Just changing his entire life's course was a lot to digest right now. He'd put his daughter first. His love for McKenzie would have to be something he carried for the rest of his life if she could never return it. And perhaps someday, it would taste more sweet than bitter. God always knew the bigger picture, and the Lord was a master healer. He would heal his heart. He would work out the best career path. If he was honest, Ben knew He already had. Ben climbed up out of the chair and gave his father a wave. "I think I'll walk down to Southern Fried Kudzu and get some lunch."

Dad winced. "The last burger I had from there was a little overdone."

Ben shrugged. "They have a new fry cook." He wondered how long before Barney would quit. He suspected it wouldn't be long. It was a shame to see the old diner lose its luster.

"Darlene told me there was a sign out front this morning."

"About what?" Ben wrinkled his forehead. When the diner closed down, he'd be hard up for a meal if he didn't make time to pack lunches in the morning.

"The place is for sale."

Ben's mouth dropped open. "Already? You're kidding. I thought—we thought—well, the rumor was that his nephew was going to buy the place."

"Apparently not."

Ben hurried out the door, hungry and curious with high hopes and his mind racing. At least this meant McKenzie might have another chance. It was what she'd wanted, and if running the diner made her happy, he'd support her, just as she had with his career and little girl. He walked rapidly down the sidewalk and crossed at the corner, waving to Claire as she slipped into the Peachtree Market. Just as his father had told him, there was a sign in the diner window announcing it was for sale. Ben barreled inside, forgetting all about hamburgers. To his surprise, Mr. Hill, much older than when he'd last seen him, was at the counter, directing employees like a traffic cop. Ben walked up to the register. "Hi, can I—" He looked through the pass-through window to the back. "Is McKenzie Price here?" Maybe she already knew.

Mr. Hill stopped issuing directions, arm dangling in the air. "No, did she say she would be?" Desperation echoed in his voice.

"I don't know." Ben hesitated. "I saw the For Sale sign in the window."

"Oh." Mr. Hill dropped his hand and stepped up to the register. He gave Ben a wistful smile.

"She was my best employee—used to talk about buying this place from me, but…"

Ben raised a brow. "I'm sure she was planning on it until your new manager arrived."

"My nephew is no longer my manager," announced Mr. Hill. His gaze shifted around the room. "The menu has been readjusted as well, and our catering options are back."

Ben grimaced. "But not your staff."

Mr. Hill swept an arm back toward the grill. "Barney is back full-time, so whatever you want."

After calling out a hello to Barney, Ben made his order and, afterward, decided to probe some more. "I think McKenzie will be excited to hear the news. She must not know."

"Oh, she knows." Mr. Hill sighed. "I called her yesterday and offered to sell to her, but she isn't interested now. She didn't want her old job back, either."

Ben's jaw went numb. "That doesn't sound like McKenzie," he said with concern.

Mr. Hill shrugged, frustrated. A few minutes later, Ben dashed out with his hot to-go bag and made a beeline for Alabaster's. Diane had offered McKenzie the temp job; maybe she'd come up with something more permanent for her. He found Diane sticking price tags on a stack of pretty gemstone earrings. "Is McKenzie here?" he panted.

Diane looked up at him with surprise. "Not right now. Is something wrong?"

"No, I—" Ben looked around in confusion, heart racing. What if she'd decided to take the job in Columbus after all? What if she didn't feel like they could be friends anymore? He swallowed. He needed her friendship. He ached for her love. Maybe coming clean would be the best way to help her move forward. Ben gulped. If he had to drive out to her place and throw himself at her feet, he would do it. Even if it meant telling her he was moving home not just for Megan and himself but for her. He'd survive if it ended in humiliation. He was getting used to that. He'd danced a hip hop routine like an idiot in front of the entire town. "Have you had lunch?" he blurted out.

"No." Diane grinned. "Dr. Cooper, are you okay? Do *you* need a doctor?"

"No, I'm fine," he said in a rush. "I thought she might be here."

"She's only part-time for the holidays, and the kids are out of school now."

"So she didn't go to Columbus?"

"Ben, what are you talking about?" Diane tossed her pin aside.

"Here, have a great day." He plopped the bag up on the counter.

"Thanks," Diane said slowly, but as he hurried through the door she called, "Hey, Ben?"

He looked over his shoulder as she said, "She's just next door."

He shook his head. "I checked."

Diane scrunched her forehead and then said, "No. Check the other way. The *other* next door, I meant."

Ben stared in confusion, but Diane went back to her work with a wisp of a smile on her lips. He let the door close slowly behind him and walked next door. The construction company had indeed closed, as Bradley had announced. The windows were blank. Ben peered in. A bare, fluorescent light bulb flickered overhead. The office walls had been dismantled. It was just a large empty room. Then his heart jumped into his throat. In the middle of it, McKenzie sat, cross-legged, on the floor. Her hair was swept up into a bun with loose tendrils floating around her face. There was a ream of paper stretched out in front of her. Ben reached for the door and swung it open, and she looked up in surprise. "Ben!"

"McKenzie. What are you doing here? I was at the diner and Mr. Hill said—"

"Hill?" She repeated with raised brows. It made her face look innocent and lovely. "He's in?"

"He's running things, by the look of things."

"Oh, poor man," said McKenzie. "Yes, he let his nephew go. Finally."

Ben put his hands on his hips, trying to sort it all out. "You aren't going to buy the diner?"

"No."

Ben dropped down onto the floor in front of her. A Christmas song crooned from her cell phone. It filled the air, making the space smaller, more comfortable. "What are you doing in here?"

"Diane decided she isn't going to expand Alabaster's."

Ben still didn't understand. "So you're moving in?" he joked, trying to keep things light.

"Yes." McKenzie looked up at him with colored cheeks. "I signed the papers this morning, and I'm now the proud owner of Books and Ivy."

Ben's breath caught in his chest, and he looked around the empty room. "What? This? Here?" His heart pattered with excitement.

She nodded with shining eyes. "Yes, thanks to you."

"Me?" Ben put a hand to his chest.

"I would have never had the courage if you didn't chase your dreams, Ben. You did everything they said you could never do."

"McKenzie," he replied, his love for her

making him glow with pride, "you're going to open a bookstore."

"Yes." She smiled faintly, then bit her lip. "But there is an escape clause.

"What do you mean?"

"I have thirty days to change my mind."

"Why would you do that?"

"Because," she said quietly, "I thought there could be a small chance that I'm moving to Ohio."

Ben's head began to whirl so fast he thought he'd topple over. "You're what?"

McKenzie climbed to her feet. She reached for his hand. "Ben, there's something you should know before you leave. I—" Her face flooded with color, eyes darkening to sapphire. "It's my turn," she said at last. "I love you. You're the best friend I ever had. I loved you then, and I love you now more than ever. You were always there for me until I pushed you away. And it was a mistake."

Ben squeezed her hand, heart soaring. They were words he'd only heard in his dreams. "I pressed you too hard back then," he murmured.

"No, you did the right thing, speaking your truth. Telling me. I was too afraid to make any commitments or to leave the only safe haven I knew. I couldn't do it then."

"You weren't ready," Ben whispered, praying she was now.

McKenzie looked at him, her face cherry red and eyes shimmering with tears. "I'm ready now. If you'll have me. There is no one in the world I want to be with but you. And I'll…" She looked around the empty shop that could become her bookstore. "I'll let this go and go with you to Ohio. If you want."

Ben pulled her to him, slowly, carefully, as if she were a delicate snowflake. He wrapped his arms around her and held his eyes closed and pressed against her forehead. "I don't want you to give this up. You don't belong in Ohio."

Her chest heaved suddenly, and a small sob escaped. Ben grabbed her shoulders and gazed into her eyes. "No, McKenzie." She squeezed them shut, and tears began to stream. He realized what this meant. She did care. She loved him. "McKenzie," he whispered, shaking her gently back into his world, "I don't want you to move to Ohio because I won't be there."

"What?" She opened her eyes and then covered her face to stall the tears.

Ben let out a nervous laugh, one full of hope and expectation. "I'm not moving to Ohio. I'm buying the clinic from my dad and selling my car," he explained, "because I need room to fit in Megan's friends."

McKenzie dropped her hands. "You're staying?"

"Yes." Ben laughed and swiped away one of her tears with his finger and trailed it down her cheek to her lips. "You love me?" he asked, heart pleading for affirmation.

"I do." She smiled weakly. "I always have, but now I'm ready to love you like you deserve." She searched his eyes. "I'm not scared anymore, Ben. I'm not buying that old diner, because it's not what I truly want. Not deep down. I never believed I could have what I wanted, so I didn't take chances. Now that I see how you've succeeded professionally and what a great father you are—I can't live the rest of my life not knowing what could have been between us." She blinked away another tear. "And I also know that even a bookstore doesn't matter more than this. Than you."

Ben couldn't hold back the exhilaration. He felt his smile stretch from ear to ear as he embraced her again, resisting the urge to jump with joy like they were kids again. "I'm not going anywhere, Mac. Merry Christmas," he whispered.

She buried her face into his neck, and her soft breath against him made him weak. "And all I got you were cheeseballs," she whispered in a muffled voice" Ben chuckled, but McKenzie insisted, "I'm serious. I wrapped them and gave them to your mom."

"Maybe we can take them up to the tree house later," he said boldly. She melted into him. Ben closed his eyes with happiness and rocked her in his arms just as the old song from their last concert began. He realized it was on her playlist, and it made his throat knot with emotion.

"Do you hear that, Dr. Cooper?" she whispered. "They're playing our song."

Ben nodded as they swayed to the music as one, holding on to each other as if they'd never let go. He realized coming home had made his dreams come true. "I'll love hearing this song at any time for the rest of my life," he promised her. "Because I'm not only home for Christmas, McKenzie. I'm home for good." He only made it one turn around the room with the woman he loved before he stopped to bend his head over hers and kiss McKenzie Price like it was yesterday. She answered like it was forever.

Epilogue

A new year. A new season. A new life. It was the perfect spring day for a ribbon-cutting in front of Books and Ivy in downtown Kudzu Creek. McKenzie took one last look around her new business with a heart full of gratitude and pride. The dark wood floors shone like mirrors. Low wrought-iron shelves were spaced evenly, creating roomy aisles. Bradley Ainsworth had built floor-to-ceiling bookshelves on either side of the room, and the small loft in the back of the store was perfect, with a tea table for board games, a shaggy luxe rug on the floor, and two beanbag chairs. The children's reading area below had an enormous tree painted in the corner, where picture books were stacked beneath it.

McKenzie inhaled the odors of paper, ink and wood polish as she stared overhead at a beautiful brass chandelier she'd bought from the antique store. Her skin seemed to buzz with joy. She was afraid if she blinked, she might wake up. It was like a dream had come to life, a world built inside her head she'd never dared believe could come true. Now, because of God's goodness, her friends and family, and her Ben, she was standing in her own bookstore. Her eyes misted, and she turned to check outside, her heart skipping a beat at the size of the crowd waiting in a line. The Chamber of Commerce was there, a few staff members from the newspaper, and all her friends and family. Bailey squashed her nose on the glass and tapped on the window, then motioned with a flapping hand that it was time. With a deep breath, McKenzie stepped outside to rejoin Jill and Ben, who was holding Megan's hand as she twirled around in circles.

"We're ready to see books!" Bailey demanded when McKenzie stepped through the door. She smiled nervously at everyone, noticing how traffic slowed as cars passed by the historic event. The sidewalks were growing thicker with well-wishers and the curious.

Laurel, president of the Chamber of Commerce, made her announcement, and the crowd clapped as the mayor cut the ribbon to Kudzu

Creek's first-ever bookstore. The throng thundered inside, many congratulating her on their way in. Last but never least, Ms. Olivia toddled up slowly, using a walker with determination. McKenzie smiled at the tinkling sound that erupted from the walker with each step. "I like the bells."

"It's so they know I'm coming," Ms. Olivia grinned. "At least the cats."

McKenzie chuckled. Behind her, Ben laughed. He stepped up and took Mrs. Olivia by the elbow. "I'm so happy to see you out and about. How about a tour by yours truly?"

"Are you working here now?" Ms. Olivia grinned "I'm here to find a book for the book club. I don't need a doctor."

"I just thought you'd need a friend."

Ms. Olivia smiled at him. "You'll always be my friend, Dr. Cooper. But I think someone else deserves your attention today."

She winked at McKenzie and let go of her walker to smooth down her wig, then clip-clopped into the store with her son at her heels. McKenzie laughed. She stepped back and watched a newspaper photographer follow the crowd in after snapping one more picture of the storefront.

Ben's arm went around McKenzie's waist.

It felt snug, safe and happy. "I'm so proud of you," he whispered. "It's beautiful."

"It's just how I imagined," McKenzie murmured back. "And adding you into the story is even better."

"Is it?" He smiled faintly.

McKenzie drew in a breath of the sweet honeysuckle on the morning breeze. "Please don't ever doubt it."

"I just wanted a moment alone."

"I'm sorry I've been busy."

Ben gave her a soft squeeze of reassurance. " "I'm proud of you. Your happy when you're busy, and I want to be a part of it."

"I want you to be a part of everything in my life." McKenzie smiled. They'd talked. A lot. The future looked bright, and with the man she loved beside her, McKenzie knew that light would never dim.

"I love you, Ben," she whispered, trembling with happiness.

He turned her to him so that they were face-to-face. "I love you, too, McKenzie. Always have. And since you've promised to love me forever, and watch over my little girl, there's something I wanted to ask you…officially."

McKenzie's breath caught in her throat.

"I don't want to make a scene," Ben whispered in her ear. "But for you, I will drop to one knee."

McKenzie looked at him in surprise until he pulled out a small bag from Knight's Pharmacy. "What's this?" she wondered in confusion.

"Something I think you need. In fact, I'm asking you to take it."

"Vitamins?" she joked. "Actually, I hope it's chocolate." Ben chuckled, but she saw the vein in his neck racing. She bit her lip and peeked inside. There was a small jewelry box, green velvet—her favorite color. With trembling fingers, she pulled it out into the cool spring air and opened it up to find a solitary square diamond. It flashed like a crystal-clear lake in the sunlight. "Just a bit of sparkle," Ben whispered, climbing to his feet, "to go with your eyes."

McKenzie's heart did a wild pirouette, and her eyes spilled over with happy tears. Her arms went around his neck before she could thank him. "A happy ending," she whispered.

"Is that a yes?"

"Is this a proposal?"

"Yes, minus an audience. It's a prescription for a happy life, where you will be the center of my world and always my first priority. Whether it's Kudzu Creek or anywhere else life takes us."

"I think Ms. Olivia would have something to say about that," choked McKenzie with laughter. She buried her face in Ben's shoulder to wipe another teardrop away, then looked into his bronze eyes glazed with emotion. "Then it's a prescription that I'm happy to take."

"Will you marry," Ben whispered.

A loud cheer of laughter echoed from inside the store. Jill was ringing up the register as fast as she could while the line began to stretch out the door. McKenzie smiled. So this was her happily-ever-after; not so far from home after all. And with the boy she'd always known belonged in her life, like her family and her hometown. "Yes, Dr. Cooper, I'll be your wife." She leaned in and tenderly kissed him, knowing Megan and Bailey would be horrified but glued to the window, nonetheless. Her concerns soon drifted off with the breeze and disappeared over the rooftops of Kudzu Creek into the bright blue sky while Ben Cooper kissed her until all she knew was utter joy.

* * * * *

Dear Reader,

Thank you for returning to Kudzu Creek at Christmastime with me. We all have dilemmas we must face in the different phases of our lives, but during the holiday season, sometimes they hit harder. That made writing McKenzie and Ben's story a sweet and reflective experience, and it sure put me in the holiday mood. We may not get much snow down South, but we still love to gather with our friends and families around the Christmas tree to stay warm and to celebrate the gifts of the heart.

I hope you were inspired by this story set in my favorite small town and reminded that life doesn't have to be perfect to love or to be loved. God knows how to mend—our broken pieces, and at Christmas He reminds us of His unfaltering love for everyone—the greatest gift of all.

If you're a new Love Inspired reader, visit my profile on Harlequin.com or checkout my website at www.daniellethorne.com for more inspirational romance and to learn a little more about me. I wish you peace this holiday season and throughout your new year.

Merry Christmas!
Danielle

Get 3 FREE REWARDS!

We'll send you 2 FREE Books plus a FREE Mystery Gift.

FREE Value Over **$20**

Both the **Love Inspired®** and **Love Inspired® Suspense** series feature compelling novels filled with inspirational romance, faith, forgiveness and hope.

YES! Please send me 2 FREE novels from the Love Inspired or Love Inspired Suspense series and my FREE gift (gift is worth about $10 retail). After receiving them, if I don't wish to receive any more books, I can return the shipping statement marked "cancel." If I don't cancel, I will receive 6 brand-new Love Inspired Larger-Print books or Love Inspired Suspense Larger-Print books every month and be billed just $6.49 each in the U.S. or $6.74 each in Canada. That is a savings of at least 16% off the cover price. It's quite a bargain! Shipping and handling is just 50¢ per book in the U.S. and $1.25 per book in Canada.* I understand that accepting the 2 free books and gift places me under no obligation to buy anything. I can always return a shipment and cancel at any time by calling the number below. The free books and gift are mine to keep no matter what I decide.

Choose one: ☐ **Love Inspired**   ☐ **Love Inspired**   ☐ **Or Try Both!**
                    Larger-Print   **Suspense**   (122/322 & 107/307
                    (122/322 BPA GRPA)   **Larger-Print**   BPA GRRP)
                                                     (107/307 BPA GRPA)

Name (please print)

Address   Apt. #

City   State/Province   Zip/Postal Code

Email: Please check this box ☐ if you would like to receive newsletters and promotional emails from Harlequin Enterprises ULC and its affiliates. You can unsubscribe anytime.

Mail to the Harlequin Reader Service:
IN U.S.A.: P.O. Box 1341, Buffalo, NY 14240-8531
IN CANADA: P.O. Box 603, Fort Erie, Ontario L2A 5X3

Want to try 2 free books from another series! Call 1-800-873-8635 or visit www.ReaderService.com.

---

*Terms and prices subject to change without notice. Prices do not include sales taxes, which will be charged (if applicable) based on your state or country of residence. Canadian residents will be charged applicable taxes. Offer not valid in Quebec. This offer is limited to one order per household. Books received may not be as shown. Not valid for current subscribers to the Love Inspired or Love Inspired Suspense series. All orders subject to approval. Credit or debit balances in a customer's account(s) may be offset by any other outstanding balance owed by or to the customer. Please allow 4 to 6 weeks for delivery. Offer available while quantities last.

Your Privacy—Your information is being collected by Harlequin Enterprises ULC, operating as Harlequin Reader Service. For a complete summary of the information we collect, how we use this information and to whom it is disclosed, please visit our privacy notice located at corporate.harlequin.com/privacy-notice. From time to time we may also exchange your personal information with reputable third parties. If you wish to opt out of this sharing of your personal information, please visit readerservice.com/consumerchoice or call 1-800-873-8635. **Notice to California Residents**—Under California law, you have specific rights to control and access your data. For more information on these rights and how to exercise them, visit corporate.harlequin.com/california-privacy.

LIRLIS23

Get 3 FREE REWARDS!

We'll send you 2 FREE Books plus a FREE Mystery Gift.

FREE
Value Over
$20

Both the **Harlequin® Special Edition** and **Harlequin® Heartwarming™** series feature compelling novels filled with stories of love and strength where the bonds of friendship, family and community unite.

YES! Please send me 2 FREE novels from the Harlequin Special Edition or Harlequin Heartwarming series and my FREE Gift (gift is worth about $10 retail). After receiving them, if I don't wish to receive any more books, I can return the shipping statement marked "cancel." If I don't cancel, I will receive 6 brand-new Harlequin Special Edition books every month and be billed just $5.49 each in the U.S. or $6.24 each in Canada, a savings of at least 12% off the cover price, or 4 brand-new Harlequin Heartwarming Larger-Print books every month and be billed just $6.24 each in the U.S. or $6.74 each in Canada, a savings of at least 19% off the cover price. It's quite a bargain! Shipping and handling is just 50¢ per book in the U.S. and $1.25 per book in Canada.* I understand that accepting the 2 free books and gift places me under no obligation to buy anything. I can always return a shipment and cancel at any time by calling the number below. The free books and gift are mine to keep no matter what I decide.

Choose one: ☐ **Harlequin**   ☐ **Harlequin**   ☐ **Or Try Both!**
                Special Edition   **Heartwarming**   (235/335 & 161/361
                (235/335 BPA GRMK)   **Larger-Print**   BPA GRPZ)
                                        (161/361 BPA GRMK)

Name (please print)

Address   Apt. #

City   State/Province   Zip/Postal Code

Email: Please check this box ☐ if you would like to receive newsletters and promotional emails from Harlequin Enterprises ULC and its affiliates. You can unsubscribe anytime.

Mail to the **Harlequin Reader Service:**
IN U.S.A.: P.O. Box 1341, Buffalo, NY 14240-8531
IN CANADA: P.O. Box 603, Fort Erie, Ontario L2A 5X3

Want to try 2 free books from another series! Call 1-800-873-8635 or visit www.ReaderService.com.

HSEHW23